TELI

Totally Amazing Little Exciting Stories

From London Vol II
Edited by Lynsey Hawkins

Dear Lucy

From your beloved Godson

Lucas Greenwood xxx

5/02/07

Disclaimer

Young Writers has maintained every effort
to publish stories that will not cause offence.

Any stories, events or activities relating to individuals
should be read as fictional pieces and not construed
as real-life character portrayal.

 Young**Writers**

First published in Great Britain in 2006 by:
Young Writers
Remus House
Coltsfoot Drive
Peterborough
PE2 9JX
Telephone: 01733 890066
Website: www.youngwriters.co.uk

SB ISBN 1 84602 655 5

Foreword

Young Writers was established in 1991 and has been passionately devoted to the promotion of reading and writing in children and young adults ever since. The quest continues today. *Young Writers* remains as committed to engendering the fostering of burgeoning poetic and literary talent as ever.

This year, *Young Writers* are happy to present a dynamic and entertaining new selection of the best creative writing from a talented and diverse cross-section of some of the most accomplished secondary school writers around. Entrants were presented with four inspirational and challenging themes.

'Myths And Legends' gave pupils the opportunity to adapt long-established tales from mythology (whether Greek, Roman, Arthurian or more conventional eg The Loch Ness monster) to their own style.

'A Day In The Life Of …' offered pupils the chance to depict twenty-four hours in the lives of literally anyone they could imagine. A hugely imaginative wealth of entries were received encompassing days in the lives of everyone from the top media celebrities to historical figures like Henry VIII or a typical soldier from the First World War.

Finally 'Short Stories', in contrast, offered no limit other than the author's own imagination! 'Ghost Stories' challenged pupils to write an old-fashioned ghost story, relying on suspense, tension and terror rather than using violence and gore.

Telling T.A.L.E.S. From London Vol II is ultimately a collection we feel sure you will love, featuring as it does the work of the best young authors writing today.

Contents

Kheshena Persaud (12)   39
Romana Khan (11)   40

Islamia Girls' School
Fatima Warsame (13)   41
Nashwa Ali (12)   42
Roheen Khan (13)   43
Bayan Cevahir (13)   44
Esma Al-Sibai (13)   45
Zahra Faiz (15)   46
Asmaa Shah (13)   47
Nabilah El-Harraj (13)   48
Ruba Ramadan (13)   49

Normanhurst School
Asim Fiaz (13)   50
Joe Woodcock (13)   51
Hannah Fullilove (13)   52
George Dew (12)   53
Rebecca Sullivan (13)   54
Charlotte Mulligan (13)   55
Oshien Sheedy (13)   56
Edward Harrison (13)   57
Ryan McDonnell (12)   58
Siobhan Wright (13)   59

North Bridge House School
Neville Rivelino (11)   60
Aodhan Buckley (11)   61
Louie Brockbank (11)   62
Joseph Sellars (11)   63
David Zhu (11)   64
Clarence Adjei-Attah (12)   65
Shayan Mahinfar (12)   66
Elizabeth Nenarokov (12)   67
Eleanor Doman (11)   68
Amy-Jane Cotter (12)   69
Anthony Cox (12)   70
Aaron Fordwoh (11)   71
Lily Grant (12)   72
Louis Merran (13)   73

Queens College

The Creative Writing

A Day In The Life Of A Slave

I am still a little girl, but I already suffered a lot in this life. I can still hear my papa's sweet voice whispering 'Goodbye Ane' with his eyes of fear opened wide at mine. My mama holding me tight and comforting me with tears rolling down her face. Those white men brutally dragged him away from me and took him to a far plantation where he would never be able to find me and my mama again.

Every day I hear his voice and I cry. They took him away and left me with a broken spirit. I miss him so much, since he's gone I am in deep pain, all I now have in this world is the love and care of my mama. We were so happy and joyful as a family but this disaster happened so suddenly.

Sometimes I wonder if I am ever going to see my beloved Papa again. I also wonder if I am ever going to be free from this devastating torture, it seems endless. Some people say freedom is impossible and hopeless. They say we were born miserable and we will die the same way.

I look around and all I see is people working day and night, suffering and getting punished without deserving it, with no way to defend themselves. Living a life of agony, being victimised by cruel white men. I have an extreme fear of losing my mama, she is all I have but she always tells me to have strength, no matter what happens, I need to remain alive.

My sweet mama told me that freedom exists in a wonderful place called Africa where there is no suffering, no torture; it is a piece of Heaven on Earth where peace and joy live. But now, Africa exists only in my mama's memory and in my imagination. I wish I could live in this gorgeous Africa with my mama and papa.

It may seem impossible but I still have this belief in my heart that one day I am going to be free. I dream about it every night and this dream gradually builds as the days pass. I know one day I will be free, by the power invested in me, I have the power and determination to be free.

Sophia Cavalcanti (15)
Capital City Academy

A Day In The Life Of An ATM Machine

I wait and wait for someone to come and insert their card. When they come, it's very funny because sometimes, depending on the card, it really tickles.

Usually people push my buttons as if they're a demented screwdriver which really annoys me so I jam the machine on purpose. If they really annoy me, I still take the money that they wanted to draw out of their card!

Sometimes, I get people that think I am a public toilet. This really upsets me, therefore the following day I pretend to be *out of order!*

If there is only a small amount of money left in my machine then I will not let anymore money out because no one likes to feel empty.

Isaac Muscatt (11)
Capital City Academy

A Day In The Life Of A Slave

(An extract)

It was pitch-black as they stored us, their *cargo*. Men, women and children crammed together like books on a shelf, on the floorboards with barely room to breathe let alone move. Stale body odour permeated the air making the atmosphere unbearable. Though my hands and legs were chained, I somehow managed to lift my upper body and as I looked to my left I could see her, *Mama!* I tried to communicate but as I did I was whipped to the floor by the white man. Deep down I wanted to retaliate but my main priority was to stay alive. As I lay onto the floorboard splinters stabbed my back but I had to bear the pain.

As I gazed up towards the black sky of the ship I couldn't help thinking to myself, *if there is a God why is He doing this to us?*

Otis Best (14)
Capital City Academy

A Day In The Life Of A Salve

(An extract)

Here I am, life is wonderful. My life is complete with everything I need. It feels like I'm in Heaven, never to be enslaved by the savage beasts, free again I wish to be. A vision I see to become true, suddenly I wake up, and realise that it was just a dream.

Freedom is all I think about, day and night. The feeling in the back of my mind of what it is to be free like the summer breeze. My mum always encourages me to lead myself to freedom and to teach the others about the motherland of Africa. I know that being free is the only wish slaves dream of, but not all of us! Some of us don't even know what it feels like to be free; their brain has been washed inside out as though it had been wiped clean through the ocean.

It was early Sunday morning, I woke up and it was a typical distressing day. I was one of the field workers who'd spend all day digging, sweeping and carrying from sunrise till sunset. Most slaves were given tasks to perform according to their physical capability. Punishment was like a daily routine for the evil white people. Not only is it physical but mental and sexual abuse are also basic parts of slavery.

I have tried to escape but it only lasted a week. They hunted me like an animal, an animal that is tortured and mentally damaged. The predators tried to wipe everything out of my head, the knowledge of my beautiful country, Africa. They even whipped, beat and drowned me almost to death but they could never break my spirit ... the spirit of being a free man.

Zolboo Badralt (15)
Capital City Academy

Juliet's Diary

I have met the most attractive and charming fellow, his name is Romeo, he has eyes of ice-blue pool and a dazzling smile which makes my heart miss a beat. I'm in love, but he is a Montague, my family's sworn enemy. I'm in such a perplexity; do I stay loyal to my kin or betray them for the love of my life? They would realise that we're intended to be together. We may have to take drastic measures if our families' reject our request, we may run away together and be married in secret, oh how romantic it would be, but I have dreamed of an extravagant wedding with all of our relations. I am optimistic yet still worried of my family's opinion, I do not want to be cut out of the Capulet family, I want my family's full consent to be with Romeo. I don't require their authorisation, but I want them to be part of my life. I could remain a Capulet by being called Mrs Juliet Capulet-Montague.

I have conversed with Romeo about what would happen in the worst case scenario, thus far, neither of us knows what would happen. Don't they love their children more than a wretched dispute? If they did they could drop the entire feud and become reunited then finally Verona could become an undivided country and there would be no more street fights and sword fights. It could solve everything.

I'll go tell the family now …

Diamond Abdirahim (12)
Capital City Academy

A Day In The Life Of Bottom

There I was minding my own business when all my friends started running away shouting, 'Bottom's got the head of an ass!' This is how it all began. I was in the forest rehearsing a play (a good one an' all) when I stumbled on a sleeping woman, but this was no ordinary woman, she had wings! Then I saw what looked like a garden gnome, he threw golden pixie dust at me. I felt a prickly sensation, I thought I was dreaming so I splashed water on my face and went to perform. That is when all the trouble began.

The fairy king came to me and told me about the joke he'd played on his wife (that was after he had let her chase me round the forest for ages) then he made me forget. It was not until an apple fell off a tree and hit me on the head did I remember. Plus the rumours and taunts are terrible; no one comes to my plays anymore.

Owen Alister-Hooke (12)
Capital City Academy

A Day In The Life Of Juliet

Juliet woke and opened her eyes; she arose from her snowy white bed and put on her silky white dressing gown. She walked down the stairs and into the kitchen; she sat down gently and was served with warm tea and carefully cut toast. After, she stood up and left her remains to be cleared up by her maid. As she got to the top of the stairs she was greeted by her mother and father. She gave them a hug and a kiss each and strolled to the bathroom, she had a long shower and after brushed her long silky hair. She made her way to the bedroom to get dressed and to choose what dress she would wear for the party she was having at the mansion that night. Her maid helped her choose between her long, white frilly dress or her red dress, it was a fancy dress party. Finally, she decided to wear her white dress so she was an angel and her mother was Cleopatra.

A while before this, the Montagues and Capulets had been fighting and set fire to a petrol station.

Later at the party, Romeo was dressed as a knight, a man called Paris was there and Juliet's parents wanted her to marry him. However, Juliet met Romeo and they got married. Unfortunately Romeo and Juliet had a tragic ending, they killed themselves and they lay together, dead, forever.

Danielle Mulqueen (12)
Capital City Academy

A Day In The Life Of Macbeth

I am in pain! Yesterday I killed the King Duncan, just as the witches said, I am now the king! Yes, OK, that is quite good but the pain of murder overloads every other emotion and movement. It feels like my clothes are being pulled down to the bloody pits of Hell, yet I still stand but it seems like I have some unfinished business.

Banquo is getting suspicious and his sons are said to be king one day. No, I can't let that happen; I have to kill them so I can carry on my reign of terror!

One of the worst things is I think I am going crazy. Today at my court I saw Banquo's spirit haunting me, all the blood, all the murder. My wife, my one true love, is lost today. Without her, life is going to be so much harder. I need her to tell me when I am going crazy, cheer me up when I get scared of visions and encourage me to do stuff I am scared of doing, like murder. Without being able to murder I'll lose my throne, no, I can't let that happen. I'll murder tomorrow, I'll tell my guards to kill Banquo and his son then there will be no challenge to my throne, after I shall go to the witches again.

Drew Davies (12)
Capital City Academy

A Day In The Life Of Juliet

'Good morning Juliet, rise and shine,' the first words I hear as I am rudely interrupted from a lovely dream by my maid. 'I'll just go and fill up your bowl with water and then leave you to get dressed.'

After breakfast, (I had toast and jam with a cup of tea) I had just settled down for another nap when I was interrupted again from my dream!

Am I ever going to get to talk to this rather handsome young chap at this ball? It feels as if it is meant to be, my destiny. (You know me meeting this handsome young chap) it feels weird!

I must admit I like this youth, he looks like the youth in my dream; I've met him at my mother and father's ball to celebrate their fortieth anniversary. To tell you the truth the whole dream is like my life, I think I heard someone call the handsome youth by the name Romeo!

Romeo and Juliet, my destiny!

Zarina Ahmed (12)
Capital City Academy

The Plain Of Tirarkonia

The dragons soared overhead slowly picking off people out of the refugee troop, but everyone kept on moving because any sign of weakness would get you killed. The people that took guns wouldn't waste any bullets on the heavily armoured dragons. Even if you tried to shoot, you would miss; you would be blinded by the sun gleaming off the blood-red scales into your eyes.

Five thousand people had set off from New Birmingham to New London but only three thousand people had made it to Tirarkonia Land where hundreds of dragons roamed, killing anyone lured in by the hope of precious dragon scales. Only the special few had the skill to reach the dragon's den where they shed their skins. The scales were used in war instead of Kevlar. Some foolish people left the troop in hope of glory and riches but they were killed almost immediately.

I rode up the side trying to keep everyone together; I was doing one of the most dangerous things on Earth. The dragons couldn't resist the thought of fresh horsemeat, and if my plan worked, they would start fighting over my horse, Flyer. Flyer was tiring, so I had doubts he could survive the lack of blood from where I had cut him to attract the dragons' attention. A dragon was closing in fast; I turned and rode towards another dragon. Being amazingly stupid the two dragons flew into each other, and started fighting because they thought they were being attacked. The other dragons joined in so I got everyone into the safer tunnel of Pabron.

Tim Whiting (12)
Capital City Academy

Nurse's Journal

Ring!

The alarm clock rang at exactly six o'clock. I slapped it and awoke reluctantly. Racing against time, I pulled on my dress and zoomed off to the kitchen to get the family their breakfast ready.

By eight-thirty everyone was at the table slurping up their tea. When Juliet was finished, she ambled off to her room as if she were hypnotised. I was worried for that little baby.

After I had cleaned up the kitchen, I sprinted up to Juliet's chamber and found her on her back. When I asked what was wrong, she replied with a sigh, 'Nurse, I think I'm in love, last night in the party I saw Romeo, we met in the backroom, eyes first, and it was so beautiful.'

I tried to make her understand that she was going to get married to Paris, but she refused and called him mean and said he had a high opinion of himself.

I actually had no idea what to do. That night I went to sleep thinking about it too. I thought I was going to let her marry Romeo. After all, she did look like my own long-lost, beloved daughter, Susan, and I would do anything just to see that smile on her face.

I decided I agreed with her and that tomorrow I was going to Lawrence to make an arrangement with him about Romeo and Juliet's marriage. I was thinking about that so much that I even dreamt about it that night. I dreamt that it was Juliet's wedding day, the Capulets and Montagues were happy again and most important of all, I saw my own Susan, she was there too, dancing with her own *Romeo*. I felt so overjoyed, I started to cry, I couldn't imagine her that grown up and merry.

Adeeba Chekeri (11)
Capital City Academy

Roots

I shouldn't have left the house to build the drum for my brother, how could I have been so foolish to disobey the rules? I'm not a man and this foolish act of mine proves it, I never would've been caught if I were one. I sat in the cage filled with burning heat pressing against me, wondering how people of my colour, my race, my country could've been against me like that, showing no remorse or guilt for the sin they are committing against me. Then I began to wonder even more, fear, pain and anger began to hit me at once, *will the others come back for me? Will I go back to my life? Will anyone care?*

I looked around to see who else had been captured; I was surprised to see Wrestler, the strongest and cleverest fighter I have seen in manhood training. Then I thought that if he, a highly thought of man that teaches those below him and is an example to us all has been captured, then surely the others must be coming for us, but a chain of doubt continued to linger through my mind. He walked towards me with his head held high as if he were trying to show that he wasn't scared and told me not to be worried. I looked into his eyes and saw that they did not give off an aura of fear but of despair and confusion.

Afterwards, white men came and forced us with guns and whips onto a ship. Thoughts of what terrors were to come ran through my mind and as I took my first step onto the ship, I wondered, *am I taking the first step to my death?* They led us down to some chambers that had flat wood as beds and chains to hold us down. Each and every one of us was chained down viciously, the white men did not seem to care if we were crying quietly or if we screamed an ear-piercing scream; they just continued their jobs like robots with no emotion.

I lay on the wood, too scared to sleep yet too frightened to stay awake, so I prayed hoping and pleading that Allah would come to my aid. I called out His name but no one replied. The same thing over and over again, the only thing I heard was the moaning, whimpering and cries of people who wished that this was nothing but a nightmare and that they would wake up, but little by little realised that they were already awake.

A stream of light shone through a hole from the stairs. It was sunlight and then the white men came and dragged us up to a higher deck. As the light hit my eyes, I was blinded for a while but I had to overcome that quickly because I had a plan to escape, I would jump in the water and swim to land. I regained my vision almost instantly and searched for land focusing completely and ignoring anything that might throw me off course. But there was no land, nothing, just water, water of the blue sea. I felt surrounded by a sea of death, and then puzzling questions washed over me, questions I didn't know the answers to and some I didn't want to know the answers to. One answer soon came to me though … I was in mortal peril!

Naide Gohar (13)
Capital City Academy

Kunte Kinte's Account

'Who are you?' I hopelessly shouted again as they threw me onto the floor, dragging me on the rough surface bruising my skin. As they lugged me onto the huge structural mechanism, I shouted like a crazy bloodhound. Bodies lay helpless across the blooded deck.

Frightened and confused yet I was *furious!* Telling myself that I am a warrior and I shouldn't be here, I should have pounded them into the ground. Shown them what a warrior can do!

I saw the vast sea of bodies which is like an ocean with many fish, caught and trapped, slowly dying. I've been here for many days but it feels like years. They take the ones who are filthy and wounded to the upper deck where they strike their bodies with the freezing, salty, ocean water burning our helpless dark skins. I realise that this is a death boat, a tomb that's trapping our race.

My plan, the only plan, was to jump overboard and swim to shore but as I studied my plan more carefully, I noticed that there was no shore to swim back to. There was only ocean in the midst of what should have been land, earth, what should have been home … feeling shattered I cried and screamed realising this was my dire destiny. The pungent stench of rancid food kept me awake. I saw vomit as it slid swiftly through the rotting wood of the deck into my mouth.

This is inhumane. This is Hell!

Ehad Ponxha (13)
Capital City Academy

A Day In The Life Of Napoleon's Sword

They were there, the English troops. My master was getting me ready and then, *slash!* I was being held by my master; he was swinging me up and down, cutting and fighting. All I saw was blood, it was everywhere and I was proud, I was proud because I was the one fighting for my country.

Suddenly, there was shouting and celebrating, we had won! Everyone shouted, 'Napoleon!' At that time I felt sad, horrendous, I'd done the work and he'd got all the credit. On that day I had lost all of my pride.

That night I was put against the wall and surprisingly, or not, Napoleon was preparing to invade England, I heard it all, but ooh as you know I'm only a sword, what can I do?

At night I couldn't sleep, just thinking about the people and soldiers that I'd killed. I wasn't proud again, I was stressed and that night I prayed!

It was the next day, I was getting ready. We were invading England; I couldn't do anything, not even move. I was stressed and then …

Igor Rodrigues (11)
Capital City Academy

The Slave Trade

It all started when I became a man. My grandma came and ruined my life. She asked me to make a drum for my brother. Meanwhile, fate made trouble for me. I went in the forest to find wood and someone found me.

I stared at the white man and his friends; I had never seen them before. I ran through the woods into a deserted field where there was nowhere to hide. I ran as fast as I could. After a few seconds I was surrounded by men who wanted to catch me. They formed a circle around me, which meant that I could not escape. At the end of this dilemma, they'd caught me.

A few hours later I found myself in a wooden house. This wooden house kept on shaking and the worst part of it was the atmosphere smelt putrid. I was chained to a wooden plank, I was not alone. I saw many people who were in the same position as me, confused.

The whole time I have been on that ship all I can think about is my family, my wonderful family. I miss my homeland, the sweet aroma of the natural air, the plain grass, the beautiful flowers I used to play with so long ago. Where am I now? I don't know, I am reduced to farmland, growing crops and helping my masters, all I want now is to go home, a home I am worthy of.

Saad Khawaja (13)
Capital City Academy

On The Ship

I am confused, where have they taken me? I can barely breathe with this rusty chain around me. My wrists and ankles feel like they're crumbling away like biscuits. I could taste the thick dust from the battered wooden floor creeping into my mouth.

The screams and cries were surrounding me; there was vomit on the floor that looked like a cow had been turned inside out. I could hear people praying for dear life. A fellow student from manhood training was getting severely beaten in a corner. The salty taste of someone's sweat slithered down my throat.

I miss my loving family, are they safe? It's my fault. I should have done as I was told. I had such a beautiful, peaceful village. I have let my family down, I've let my teachers down and I've let myself down.

I can feel my life sweeping away, my heart sinking and my soul starting to crack. My family must be ashamed. I must be strong and brave, I can't just give up. I will fight for my family and friends. I've become a warrior and I will die like one, fighting for freedom.

I will attack the guards once they've let me free and then make a break for freedom, I must believe in myself. They have unchained me! My heart leaps into my throat, my blood rushes to the top of my head, my legs freeze and I become unbelievably weak, here goes nothing!

Enes Dizdarevic (13)
Capital City Academy

Deep Thoughts

I have housed many prisoners in my dark walls. Ever since the time of William the Conqueror when I became this sombre, murky tower, this tower that everyone loathes and dreads. For in my cradle do skeletons hang, bodies rot and carcasses melt into a meagre powder. But this place is not without its excitement. There is the hunger of people's feelings, their screams and sorrows, the beseeching letters they write pleading for forgiveness. Indeed, the human lust for life will never cease.

But today, today is different. Today I have a new quest, a new victim. Of course, it's not as though I devour them but they really do perish. Today, there's a young girl. She has pale skin, red hair, blue eyes and a serious expressions. She is intelligent, you can tell. Her name is … Elizabeth. She's a princess and a Protestant. That is dangerous in these times and she knows this but she pretends that she's a Catholic because she's scared of her sister who will surely kill her willingly enough.

My new protégé is frightened, frightened to the bone that she'll be beheaded, just like her cousin. However, you have to feel sorry for her, her mother beheaded, her father who ignored her, a kindly stepmother who had loved her yet the foolish actions of a man turned her stepmother's love into hate and jealousy.

She walks around my staircases feeling my dark, forbidden depths with her fingertips. She has heard stories of ghosts and spirits, of two princes that died in my tower, their remains somewhere here. Her breath catches and her body stiffens as she hears a crack, a bang and a fall.

There are footsteps tapping the cold stones of my floor, hurried footsteps, thudding like a damp, suffocating heartbeat. Here comes my second protégé, I love his rasping, cracked voice as he says, 'Who's there?'

Amina Seylani (12)
Capital City Academy

A Day In The Life Of Clouds

I am always up there watching you move around, jump around, roll around, just generally seeing you move around the place. There are always people moving around and I am always there, above you, watching you and you don't even notice me.

When I'm watching, I always see your head, sometimes you have a hat on, sometimes you have dandruff on your hair and sometimes you're just bald. You don't realise I see you so try to keep your head clean because you never know who's watching.

Actually I see everything that goes on. I see people shopping, eating, playing or even crying. I don't understand why you're always doing something why can't you just be still like the statues you make?

It will be much easier for you, try it because you never know who's watching. On certain days in the year, I look down and see people celebrating special occasions. I don't really know what you're celebrating or why you bother to celebrate. What good does that do you? Stop because you never know who's watching.

Last, but definitely not least, I see people dying, hurting. Why do people die? I don't understand. Every day someone dies, or someone gets hurt or gets a beating. Why can't you just get a job to earn money instead of mugging helpless people? Stop, because you never know who's watching!

Mahmud Ndanusa (12)
Capital City Academy

A Day In The Life Of A Bin Outside Selfridges

For ten years I've been considering giving my life story to you, the people of the world. Now I've finally decided that I am going to share my interesting life story with you, so here it goes.

Well, as I've been living here for ten years I am very familiar with loud pumping pop music that is always coming out of that massive shop. It used to be fine, as me and my old mate Bingy used to just listen to it. But now he's gone, he was removed and destroyed because of the London bombings, I hate it because the music's changed, it's not like it used to be, nice and slow, now it's always loud pop music.

Right, if you didn't like me moaning about the noise you're certainly not going to like me complaining about littering. Well, let's see, when was the last time someone littered right in front of me? Oh yeah, it was two minutes ago! The littering around here is so atrocious that someone is probably littering every ten minutes.

Here's something else to moan about, the disgusting perfume smell that comes out of Selfridges. I mean we're bins, we can't stand those disgusting smells, I wish a dog would just poo on me!

Now I've finally got something happy to talk about, the lovely window displays. Oooh, aren't they so beautiful and interesting? I wish I could live in the windows with those lovely dummies.

Now one last moan about those horrible mean drunks who go around kicking me, they also spit and shout at me!

Now you've heard about my wonderful interesting life now, so bye-bye!

Gus Jones-Donelly (12)
Capital City Academy

Living Pain

I sat on the side of the master's well polished balcony watching the ball of red-hot fire go to a rest. Every night, I would sit at this particular place after I finished cooking and cleaning for the master's only daughter Mary. Hoping that one day I would find out who my real daddy was.

I could hear my dad calling my name, I know he's not my really daddy but the thought of being a rapist's child, a product of rape, just feels like someone is tearing my heart up into a million pieces.

'Elizabeth,' he shouted, with a fuming sound in his voice. I knew the master was over by our cabin. I think the master knows I'm his child, that's why he favours me above all the other children slaves.

My mother always tells me that I should never cry when I see or hear the white folks, torturing and putting us black slaves under unbearable pain because they can only touch our bodies but they can't touch our souls. That's why I don't shed any tears when I know he's trying to take away my mum's dignity.

Early this morning, around five, all the slaves were woken up to go and have some food before they started working on the field. The way they feed the children of my kind is horrifying, they treat us like animals. Mostly like pigs. Healthy eating is not something that we black slaves are used to. We desperately gather around our muddy wooden bowls knowing this will be the only food we'll eat for the entire day. My body feels weak and dirty but at the same time satisfied.

The word 'living' means nothing to me but following orders day after day. Working on the field in the hot weather, being violated by the hot-tempered slave driver who whip us for standing up to him. People like me aren't allowed to learn how to read or write and if we do learn how to do these things, the slave masters will beat the very skin off our backs, then sell us. *Sell us.* We are their property.

Tresan Malcolm (14)
Capital City Academy

Life As A Slave
(An extract)

I remember, yes, I remember the stories Mama and Papa used to tell me about Africa, the motherland, before the white man came and captured and separated our family. Yet me, Kofi, that's my African name but now known to the white man as Michael, was born and raised into slavery. Yes, that's right born and raised into slavery. I've never tasted the air of freedom. I've been here all my life and I still don't even know if I am coming or going.

Guess what? I've got an idea, I'm going to escape from this plantation and get to the north side where it's safe and try and find Mama and Papa, that's if I remember their faces. It's a great plan; I can't wait until I see freedom. I wonder how it is, I wonder how it feels, that feeling just makes everything come to a standstill and it feels like I'm the only person in the world, but on the other hand just imagine if I got caught. What would happen to me? They might just torture me and leave me for dead. I have to take a gamble, I must do it if I want to make it to the safe side and live a healthy and slave-free life. OK, I'm going to grab everything I can and tonight I'm off!

There I was in my little compartment thinking, *shall I, shall I not?* Walking up and down while my heart was beating as the same as each footstep. Fear taking over my mind, walking up and down the room thinking so hard that it gave me a headache, my head felt like it wanted to explode like a bomb.

Finally I gathered enough courage and set out in seek of the north, viewing my surroundings cautiously. Step by step, hoping no one had seen me, I saw my opening into the woods, I crept into the dark forest and made a run for it not looking back, just focusing on the path ahead, and thinking about the consequences of getting caught by the white man.

Effy Abbe (15)
Capital City Academy

A Day As A Flower

I was sitting there watching the people go past in the park. It was a sunny day and everyone came out to see all the beautiful flowers and the lakes. Suddenly, a group of visiting people came and were looking at me, surprised at how beautiful I was and how good I smelt. However, they left because it started to get cold and windy. No one came back and the park looked very empty with no one looking at the beautiful thing in the park. I started to feel lonely after a week.

The wind blew so hard that it swept me away from my place and my home into another country far away from my friends and family. I started crying because I knew no one and my family wasn't with me. Then when I landed on the wet ground someone picked me up and smelt me. They were surprised at how beautiful I was and how good I smelt.

Luckily the person who got me loved flowers and took me home and put me in a vase. The next week I saw how the person liked to watch TV and choose different clothes each day of the week. It was such fun watching everyone in the house and their guests.

The next day I remembered how much I missed my friends and family. I started crying and crying. I didn't eat anything and then all of a sudden, I didn't breathe or do anything and so I died.

Ancuta-Raluca Lupascu (12)
Capital City Academy

Fortunate Escape

Freedom is a dream which every single black man dreams about in this malicious state. A dream when a black man can feel that he has the same rights as a white man. He can drink from the same tap as a white man, he can read and write the same as the white man, but this isn't happening yet. Black men are still being tortured to death, women are still being sexually humiliated in front of their husbands, for black people, life is being made hell. To prevent these oppressions and the degradation from happening then the only option available is to escape.

Omar Bin Al-Sayied, the grand name I was titled, has been taken away and has been replaced by the white man's name, William. I was a well renowned trader in Africa and Asia where I traded for twenty-five years. I am well-educated in one of the most civilised countries of Africa, Nigeria. In both of the continents I was treated with such dignity and respect but here, that admiration doesn't exist anymore. The power is in a white man's hands and he can do anything he wants to.

Mr John Alex is the owner of this vast-stretched plantation that I am in. He is one of the most racist and belligerent slave holders I've ever seen. Whenever his anger arises, he takes it out on the poor, helpless slaves, especially on young boys, tormenting them till near death.

It's two o'clock in the hot summer afternoon and the sun is shining right above my head. All of the other slaves are scattered around the plantation, like convoys of ants hunting for their survival.

For how long do I need to withstand this brutal pressure? I am not allowed to practice my religion; I am not allowed to have a conversation with anyone. What is more exhausting is that I need to wake up at four o'clock in the morning, walk for an hour to reach the plantation and then take about twenty-five minutes to get to my position in the field, and dig for up to fifteen hours. Would any white person volunteer to do that? The answer would certainly be *no!*

I am full of hope for tonight, there is a bit of fear, so there is motivation for the future. I've waited for this day for a long period of time. I made a final decision and that resolution is I need to make an escape today because Mr John Alex will be holding a banquet with his fellow companions. Everyone will be busy dancing and singing, the guards will be busy, so this is a special opportunity of a lifetime not to be missed.

The future is full of happiness, pride and freedom. Free from the dreadful torture and degradation of the white man. Life will be such a relief like a free flying bee in paradise. What lies ahead of me will be full of joy and passion but the unbearable pain which I've suffered and the lonely, depressed people of Africa will helplessly remain in my heart, having hope, eagerness and determination for my people to be set free and treated equally will always be my dream.

Abdul Haseeb Seylani (15)
Capital City Academy

A Day In The Life Of A Slave

The sun shone upon my broken window and I thought to myself that another day like hell has begun. As the sunrays were revealed towards me I opened my eyes and swivelled my body, I saw my belligerent master in my bed. I, naked, powerlessly got myself out of the bed and hid my flesh from the world.

Having been born with no identity, no power, no rights and no relatives except a single depressed mother who is dilapidated but yet still tries to placate and comfort me. Born from the same man who now uses me as a sexual toy and grown up by the same mother who was once used in the same way. How could anyone's god allow such evilness and demoralisation? My only power, hope, and personality my broken-spirited mother, through whom I visualise the freedom, humanity and anticipation that if not us, may it be our children who will live life peacefully in an equal community.

A living hell plantation where life and death means the same, where violation, fear and the unbearable pain stays the same every day. Treated no different to pigs, cows and fed no better than wild birds who hunt all day for a single little piece of thrown away food to survive on. Our black dark chocolate skins are tortured, whipped, ravaged all day long whereas we suffer the humiliation, loneliness and depression in the extensive dark nights. The brutal traumatic punishments by the vicious white men have filled the everyday events in the lives of us slaves.

Having been brainwashed, neglected and defenceless in prison and matured in the unchanged place, witnessing people coming and escaping but I have not seen the world outside, have not felt the emotions of freedom and relief. Unknowledgeable about my name, religion and language, however being called Stacey, an American Christian name, is my only identity and though I speak the language of others around me, forcibly makes me one of them. Being four months pregnant and giving birth to children of a person whom I was born from, is an excruciating and horrifying experience but how long ... how long will God be watching us suffer?

Tormented, lynched and dishonoured is not unusual but living in constant fear of being sold away from my anxious mother is my major fear, for I live in this hell and helplessly go through the horrendous nightmares and agonising devastation. The short but yet long seventeen years of my life have been full of depression and humiliation. My dreams, my only strength and privacy in which I think of happiness, power and pride for us blacks but when and how the future will decide.

As the sunrays disappear the cold darkness in the huge sky indicates traumatic deeds that lay ahead. The sun has done its job but in peace, unlike us enslaved blacks getting tortured, offended and worn out despite the fact that for many, this is their last day together and many may not be reunited. While I fearfully enter my bedraggled room, praying for a peaceful night, I open the door which conceals the outrageous actions in the room. I notice my father and master sitting on my bed waiting for my presence and I am aware of the anxiety, disgrace and brutality that will follow tonight ... yet again.

Jameel Shah (15)
Capital City Academy

A Day In The Life Of A Slave

'Elizabeth! Elizabeth!' I heard my name being called. I opened my eyes gradually not wanting to break the gorgeous dream, but finally I opened drowsy eyes, the warm sunshine welcomed me with a smile. I heard my mother calling me again. Yes, my mother, I am extremely lucky to live with my mother and father, Mary and George; I love my parents. They taught me about paradise called Africa, a glory I've never seen but in fact I hear about it in such a ghastly way by Master John. My papa tells me that Master has never seen the heaven of Africa, if he did, he would never speak in that way. Every night I dream myself in Africa with freedom, with no one in charge, just me and me, only the dream gives me the strength for the next day just thinking one day my dream will come true. Every day is a desperate struggle, a struggle full of pain and misery for me and every other slave.

I see black slaves working as hard as machines but still getting tortured, it rips my heart which cries tears of blood, tears of unbearable pain and cruelty. This question spins in my brain like a tornado, were we born to suffer the bleakness of white men? The life in plantation is just like a nightmare, a terrifying dream that no one can visualise!

As I step out of the door of my so-called house, a house which is nothing compared to the master's house, I look at the house and heave a sigh and pray to God to twist my days, the days I wish for, the days I dream of. Deep inside my heart I know that one day I will be free, free like the breeze. I walk to the plantation heavy-hearted to give a hand to my mama who is continuously stacking sticks for the fire. I hear a scream, a scream which petrifies me. I run towards the scream and see a young man hanging on a tree and getting thrashed. I recognise the face, it's Tommy who went to an unknown destination to hunt for freedom, the freedom which is running away from us day by day, a freedom you can chase and be fortunate enough to catch. This young man chased it but was tripped over by the barriers of white men. God knows how many escaped and how many accomplished gaining a fresh life.

Sundus Rizvi (15)
Capital City Academy

My Mafia

I stood up, nervously looking at the other students in the class I walked to the front of the classroom dragging my feet - I had been dreading this moment, the moment when I presented to the class my family history.

I took a deep breath; the history teacher looked at me expectantly. 'My great-grandfather was Alberto Machino. He was born in Italy in 1891 into a rich family, one of the most notorious in Italy. This was because of its gangster dealings, if you didn't show them respect you would probably be shot and found in a dumpster the next week. My ancestors were part of the Italian Mafia. My grandfather was born in 1932 and when he was ten, his father was shot. From that day on he wanted to leave his criminal family but he never got away. Then, my father was born in 1965 and at the age of fourteen he immigrated to Britain and married my mum,' I paused. 'One of his wedding vows was to never have dealings with the Mafia again and he never broke his promise.'

This wasn't strictly true. I thought about the four bodyguards at my sister's wedding and the time when he taught Richard, my twelve-year-old brother how to put together a machine gun, not to mention the fact that there are two bodyguards patrolling our house - but I wasn't going to tell my class that.

I walked back to my seat, feeling relieved and thinking, *thank God that's over,* and that was when the first bullet smashed through the window.

Nina Fletcher (13)
Hornsey School for Girls

Teenager Home Alone

Jenny,

I am at my poetry club; this may be the reason why I'm not at home talking to you. If you feel lonely at all, feel free to invite a select few of your fellow pupils to revise or do your homework. Try not to break anything, darling. If you and your friends can think of anything associated with Edgar Allen Poe's 'The Raven' then please write it on this post-it.

Your mother.

Mum, look at this neon post-it note stuck on the fridge.

I am writing this letter slowly because you can't ready very fast. There was no food in the house except vodka and toast. I tried making an alcoholic version of French toast but to no avail, because apparently alcohol and stoves do not appreciate each other. I will just leave the toast and the dirty dishes in the sink. And the singed oven gloves.

Me and my friends had a 'get-together' and half the school came. I hope you won't be too mad that your vase is broken. We were playing tennis in the dining room. It had the word Lalique on the bottom of it so I just assumed it was some cheap French brand. My friend is a anarchist and he suggested we move my drum kit into the garden so we could play as a protest against President Bush. Mr Jenkins from number nineteen seems like a very reasonable man, says he won't press charges.

Jenny.

PS birds?

Romany Ghani (13)
Hornsey School for Girls

The Day I Saved My Grandmother

It was a lovely summer day in Texas, USA. I was six years old. Me and my grandmother were making dinner for the rest of the family who either had gone to work or shopping. We were making rice with chicken. I helped to make the dessert which was ice cream with jelly. After a while my grandmother really needed to go to the toilet, she walked upstairs but didn't get far because she fell onto the landing. I ran upstairs to see what had happened and I helped her up and went back downstairs to watch television. After a while my grandmother did not come downstairs and the house was really quiet.

I decided to go upstairs and nearly screamed at the sight, my grandmother had collapsed! I tried to pull her into the bedroom, but she was too heavy, so I had to run all the way to my neighbour's house that my grandmother was quite good friends with. I told her what had happened and she called 911. I ran back to my house and waited for the ambulance. They came and took her along with me and her neighbour.

When everyone found out what had happened they ran to the hospital. Everyone praised me for doing the right thing and my grandmother was OK. At least I got my ice cream!

Azra Aghil (12)
Hornsey School for Girls

The Missing Cat

As the sun set in the evening and the rain came down there was still no sign of Felix.

'Mum, where could Felix be?' cried Anna.

'I don't have a clue where that cat Felix gets to darling,' replied Mum.

Suddenly, a big gush of wind came in and left the window swinging.

'It's getting very windy,' said Mum as she shut the window.

Anna was so worried about Felix she kept popping to the toilet.

'Mum, can we please go out and find Felix?' asked Anna.

'Anna, Felix will come home when he's ready as cats always do,' said Mum.

'But, what if someone's taken him?' cried Anna.

Then there was a knock at the door, it was Justin. Justin was a friend of Wendy, Anna's mum.

'Hello Wendy, hello Anna,' said Justin.

'Hello Justin,' said Wendy and Anna at the same time.

'What's the matter Anna?' asked Justin.

'Someone's taken my Felix,' replied Anna.

'Who's Felix?' asked Justin.

'Felix, he's my cat,' replied Anna.

'Don't worry, Felix will come back when he's ready,' said Justin.

Soon Mum prepared dinner for everyone, when the food was made they sat down to eat. Whilst they were eating they heard a sound. Anna went to see where it came from. Just as Anna opened the front door she heard a miaow, it was Felix.

'Hooray! Felix has come home at last,' shouted Anna as she hugged the dripping cat.

Munmeet Manget (12)
Hornsey School for Girls

A Bad Day For St Anthony's Football Club

St Anthony's Club are the best club in Twailand. They had football clubs, swimming, reading, sleepover and lots of other clubs. All the town's children went there.

St Anthony's football club had a game to play with Kano boys. Their top goal scorer was at home practicing, their goalkeeper was with him, they were best friends, their names were Joseph and John. After practicing for an hour-thirty minutes, Joseph tried to kick the ball into the net but tripped and fell on his leg. He started groaning, crying for help. John had already ran to call Joseph's mother. She ran and called the ambulance. They took Joseph into the hospital, they examined him and found out he had broken his leg. It was only an hour before the game started.

John told the rest of the team, Joseph was in the audience. The game began, Joseph was not happy. After the first half the score was 2-2. It was now second-half, it ended 2-2. Joseph was still worried. Penalty shots ended 6-5 to Kano. Kano boys had won and Joseph was sad.

Comfort Ajoku (12)
Hornsey School for Girls

Behind The Hidden Door

'Well this is it,' Mum said quite stressfully.

'Yeah, this is it, the dumping ground,' I replied.

'Oh, why are you always so negative Saffire?'

'Um … I dunno Mum maybe … cos I want to? Let's get in then,' I boomed.

Well when they said they'd be moving us into a mansion they really meant it. 'I'm going to unpack,' I said creaking upstairs. I started to unpack when I heard the tap running in the room next to mine. I peeked my head around the corner and … *oh my God,* it was a dark figure. It was running after me, I tried to scream but nothing was coming out. I locked myself in my room. Next thing you know it zoomed straight at me. I tried attacking it but the object went straight through me. 'I'm scared, leave me alone,' I cried.

'I'm not going to hurt you, I always travel from house to house. I'm friendly.'

'Oh thanks for not harming me, do you think we could be friends?'

'Of course, I don't get many friends round here.' And from that day we formed a close friendship.

Jenny Janes (12)
Hornsey School for Girls

The Candle Of Flame

The enchanted smell envelops the room, there in the serene room sits a candle waiting to light itself up so I can tell its story from the past. To tell its story it must light up, now it can be told, the candle of flame.

It was a shivering night, a candle called Lavender sat at the side of a street lighting the way with her flame. A man walking on the street spotted Lavender; he picked her up and took Lavender to his ancient shop.

When Lavender got into the shop she was placed near the window. Lavender was surrounded by candles; all the candles had the same colour and scent, except Lavender.

'Look! Have you seen Lavender with the eyesore colour and the unpleasant smell?' sneered Vanilla One. 'Lavender should envy our vanilla scent.'

Lavender overhead, her light dimmed. She wished she could be like the other candles, instead of being proud of who she was.

A man named Kinston came into the shop, he was looking for a special candle, he saw Lavender, picked her up and sniffed her. 'Oh the aroma!' exclaimed Kinston. Lavender heard her praise, she started to brighten up. Kinston bought Lavender.

On the day of the banquet, Lavender was placed in the middle of the candelabra to flourish. Surrounding her were candles, Lavender realised that all the candles had different features, they were unique. 'Being unique being yourself makes people respect who you are, even twins can't be unique,' proudly said Lavender.

Ruth Dede Omenyo (12)
Hornsey School for Girls

My Ultimate Plan To Get Dan

Here it is, the day I'm going to ask Dan out. He is the kindest, finest boy in the whole world. OK! OK! He is sixteen and I'm only thirteen.

Ring! Ring! went the doorbell. Slowly he walked out and his beautiful green eyes stared down at me.

'Yes!' his deep voice grunted.

'I was … um … wondering if … um … we can go out … um tomorrow night?' I said sounding desperate.

'You! You're way too young for me.' He slammed the door in my face and left me standing there upset. But I had a plan! I was getting a makeover!

That afternoon I asked my sister to give me a total makeover to make me look eighteen. After the makeover I looked like a girl with a scruffy blonde wig, with red high heels and a red glittery dress. My face was covered with make-up and bright red lipstick, I thought it was convincing enough to make him say yes.

The night came very quickly; I struggled to walk to his door. As I rang the doorbell a gorgeous-looking boy answered. 'Hi, my name is Jessica, I was wondering if you would go out with me?' I asked. Dan saw right through me and said *no* in an angry deep voice. I thought that I would never go out with an older boy, ever in my life!

Jeanette Akinboyewa (12)
Hornsey School for Girls

The Horror Of A Brother And Sister

As me, Sally, and my brother, Andy sit in the pouring rain with only a cardboard box to protect us and a McDonald's cup full of coppers but not enough to buy bread, people are passing by and only shaking their heads at us and maybe feeling sorry for us. We don't know much, all we know is that we don't have a mother or father to comfort us, we were abandoned when I was five and my brother was three, we've been living on the streets for four years now.

We starve and cry ourselves to sleep. Once the police appeared right before us, oh how scared we were, they gave me and my brother a Happy Meal each, my brother took it in as fast as possible but I told him that we would have to save some for dinner and for the next day.

When I was young I had written stories and poems so I decided that the next time I saw a police officer I would hand them to him and maybe, just maybe, me and my brother would become rich and stop living on the streets.

Sandra Tawiah (12)
Hornsey School for Girls

Lost In The Unknown

I'm lost in this unknown place; I'm inside something dark, without life. I can hear the wind blowing and the birds singing, but what's happened to me? I can't remember anything, maybe … except for I was attacked, by a vampire and I might have just killed my best friend! I can remember that I was attacked by a vampire, of course. In the night the moon was shining, I was walking down the street then suddenly something bit me on my neck, it was tall and had a long shadow with fangs. I was bitten by it deep on the neck, and it left two marks with blood coming out. I had to kill someone to survive, I must suck their blood. I will suck the next person who comes along and guess who came, Sky, my best friend! That day I murdered her. I think I know what I'm stuck in, regret, if only I could travel back in time, I would change the past! A tear drops from my face, then another *drip, drip* …

Suddenly, a light came up, then another, all of a sudden all of the lights lit up! What is happening? But now I can see clearly, I'm stuck in an engine, something, something that looks like a travelling machine. Since I can travel back in time, I go back to the past and I can see myself attacking Sky, I quickly push her away so I am attacked again and so I kill myself!

Zhilin Jiang (12)
Hornsey School for Girls

The Weirdest Thing

It was an ordinary Saturday. I was hoping to go out and hang around with my friends but I couldn't. It was pouring down with rain so I stayed indoors with my mother who was busy doing her housework and I had no homework. After lunch I was sitting in the living room thinking what to do when all of a sudden a thunder wave came crashing into the cliff and I was sitting in the middle of the cliff surrounded by a little rock and sea, every time the wave came in it took a piece of the rock on the cliff away.

My heart was thumping like mad. I was sitting in the middle of nowhere screaming my head off, but then I thought to myself, *no one can hear me!* Then after at least half an hour of me being in the middle of nowhere I was sitting on a tiny piece of rock. *I am finished*, that was all that was going through my head then the next wave came in hitting the rock with all its force. Before I could say another word I realised I was falling … it was so high that I couldn't even see the ground then I landed with a great big thump! I opened my eyes looking around and saw I was on the floor of my living room … I'd been dreaming!

Kheshena Persaud (12)
Hornsey School for Girls

Amber And Karey, The Teen Detective Twins

Amber and Karey were reading their favourite Sherlock Holmes book at the company where their dad worked.

'Argh, somebody help!' Everybody ran to the source of the scream. 'Somebody's stolen my platinum watch!' cried Mrs Revelle (Dad's boss.)

'What did you hear?' someone asked.

'Well, all this happened ten minutes ago when there was a power cut, all I heard was a stomp, stomp, stomp and a swipe but I didn't realise my watch was stolen until now.'

Amber thought to herself, *I went to the loo in the other department ten minutes ago but there wasn't a power cut. Which means it was only this block, so the blackout was planned! It must have been done by an experienced person.* Amber and Karey who were thinking exactly the same, both uttered the same word, 'Electrician!'

They explained their notion to everybody in the room. They found the electrician's name was Sheikh.

'That's why he was looking so suspicious,' somebody said.

'And it explains the stomp, stomp as well, it's the DMs he always wears,' said another.

The electrician stormed into the room. 'Mrs Revelle, I think I've caught the thief!'

'Give it up Sheikh, you've been found out!' Amber and Karey said simultaneously. Within thirty minutes the police arrived at the scene and brought the thief to justice. Amber and Karey were awarded three-hundred pounds worth of Hamley's vouchers; Mrs Revelle said she had to get rid of them anyway!

Romana Khan (11)
Hornsey School for Girls

Miserable Me

School was a misery. I got picked on because of my illiteracy and because I didn't wear the right sort of clothes. My worn jeans I'd wore since the beginning of the year were my only pair.

Home life was also unbearable. I had chores to do everything. Madame Wentworth owned me and she hit me for the slightest thing. I wasn't allowed to eat much but the others ate mouth-watering meals and scrumptious savouries. Sometimes when Madame was out I ate the children's leftovers, savouring them.

Today was the worst day ever. The whole class ganged up on me, they chanted, 'You stink!' this was true but to hear this from others was hurtful.

As I trudged home the sun blistered my painful back. The sky looked wonderful, the trees swayed as if they were living a life of calming music. The birds chirped happily. I thought to myself, *why isn't my life like this?*

When I arrived home Madame was carrying a spoon and bottle. 'Open your mouth!" she ordered, I opened my mouth when suddenly I was in agony, my tongue was burning. I ran to my box room, packing my ripped schoolbag with essential needs, I sneaked through the back door. I'd made my decision; I would be a street child.

Fatima Warsame (13)
Islamia Girls' School

Life Or Death

I sprinted like a gazelle being hunted by its predator, in my case it was a single-minded heartless murderer. My heart beat faster than a baby and a tear slid down my face as I thought this would be one of my last moments. My eyes continuously scanned what was in front of me keeping me alert. I was panting uncontrollably wanting to stop but knowing I couldn't let myself be defeated. I was shivering with fear and the wind hit my face like a barrier not letting me pass. I ran, my motivation fighting with the force of the wind. I ducked, I swerved, I narrowly avoided bumping into a tree and a boulder. I was continuously swerving and ducking, thinking of an obstacle course where there was a winner and loser but for me it was a matter of life and death. If I was defeated there would be no longer be a Carmencita.

I started having hope that I might escape but I could see no way out. I was trapped in endless amount of trees, like the endless forest. Then a branch seized me by my hood and held me tight in its grip, not letting me go, like a mother seizing a child when it tries to get away. The branch was giving advantage to the murderer. I vigorously tugged, every second was precious, it could make a massive difference. I carried on but there was a thunderous, crackling sound. For the first time I stopped, the rain would definitely slow me down, the thunder howled with laughter at my misfortune.

I was drenched and started crying. I wished I were in the comfort of my house where I would only read about chases, not endure them. Then something grabbed me suddenly with all their might, so violently, I nearly tripped! My heart skipped a beat, had my time come? I looked up apprehensively at the thing grabbing me.

After that day I was never seen by any human because I was no longer a living creature.

Nashwa Ali (12)
Islamia Girls' School

Bullet

I crouched on my knees as another bullet flew past my shoulder; it was so sudden I was sure all living things around us had been awoken.

I soon realised he was getting better; shortly I would have nowhere to hide, nowhere to take refuge. My mind was isolated for a second as my body was paralysed. I lost balance. Hopelessly my lump of a body fell to the ground as there was nothing more to support me. The ground as cold as an ice rink was merciless, it felt like it was sucking my face from beneath its surface. My jaw momentarily cracked and unleashed from its nooks. The teeth I once had were now scattered in minute pieces like beads from a bracelet whose string had been cut. I was more like a bracelet too, my lifeline had been cut and I was scattered in pieces on the floor. Blood rushed to be set free from all openings I had now obtained. I was, as I realised, beyond repair. I knew that my soul was no longer in contact with my body.

I had failed my mission on Earth. My journey was now left incomplete. I was to go on bravely, I had heard the chief say and so I will. But where? This I was about to find out …

Roheen Khan (13)
Islamia Girls' School

The Time Has Come!

I'd never thought I'd end up like this, face to face with death, my eyes big, red and swollen, trying to make a difference in life.

Then he looked coldly at me, dressed in all black and I could see nothing except red, bloody eyes and him saying to me, 'Your time has come.'

At that moment I was scared, really scared and I began to think of all the things I have ever done. Hypocrisy and lying came to my head at first, then the rest began popping up. I looked at him and shouted, 'Show me all the good things I have done! There were too many, too many to count!'

Then he bent down on his knees and told me to look up. As I gently moved my head upwards, I saw a powerful bright light. I quickly turned to him and saw his arm pointing at the light. He looked at me and said, 'That's where you belong!'

As I took a step in it my eyes began to water, water like the beautiful waterfall surrounded by white Siberian tigers. It was as clear as crystal and I could see my amazing green eyes reflecting in it. I was surrounded by green with millions of soft, velvety petals on a maroon-ripe rose. I felt relaxed as if breathing in peace. It smelt of a beautiful, strawberry fragrance which brought back happy times, making me feel perfect as if I had been born again.

Bayan Cevahir (13)
Islamia Girls' School

A Special Person

She was lying there smiling as if her job was done. She lit up the room with a shimmering and glowing face. Her soft and calm eyelids at peace. Her hands softly placed by the side of her. From where the wise words that her lips spoke, now rested. Her body giving off a sweet and serenifying smell of musk. The love that she shared with her family and son, the patience she dealt with during the times she was most tested, the great knowledge and wisdom she passed onto others and her great faith that she practiced each day and night, each grew her stronger and built her character.

Now, at last she had reached the stage of happiness and comfort, where her soul could drift away with the many memories she lived with. Her great personality forces oneself to remember her in our hearts for evermore. And now she is happy, happy that the first chapter of her life has just ended - and the second has just begun.

Esma Al-Sibai (13)
Islamia Girls' School

Light

In the dark I had been running really quickly, like a jaguar from an image which I thought was a ghost but I couldn't tell as there was no light. I was running in all directions away from it, left, right, up, down, round and round. Finally, I've lost track of it, like a train with no driver as the train hasn't got a clue of where it's going. Soon I thought I'd escaped and was now free ... but a really heavy hand which probably weighs a tonne gripped onto my shoulder and it felt like my soul came out and back in again like a bouncy ball.

As I was turning in small motions to see what it was, my whole body from head to toe was shivering and shaking like a rattle. As I could see who it was, my eyes opened in a flash and *phew* thank God it was a dream!

I jumped out of bed and could see everything so clearly. The sun was beaming right into my eyes and sparkled them up like a flash bulb. I was crying with happiness to see light around me. It was like a precious jewellery box with loads of fragile happiness in it.

I realised that you should always be proud of what you have and not be finicky. As the hours, days, weeks, months and years passed by, I wondered day by day what the ghost represented!

Zahra Faiz (15)
Islamia Girls' School

The Kidnap

Once there lived a very rich man named George Kent who was the richest man in his country and was happily married with an adorable girl, Elizabeth. They lived in an exquisite mansion with six floors, a gigantic swimming pool and a breathtaking view.

Mr Kent was a tall, elegant man with a big heart. He had a very neat and short haircut with a small moustache. He wore a clean white shirt with a small black waistcoat, covered by a long black tailcoat and pitch-black trousers. He also had a very shiny pair of shoes, a long grey Kashmir coat, a posh walking stick and a tall black top hat.

Elizabeth Kent was born in Royal hospital as a cute chubby baby. Once she had come home, Mr Kent took her everywhere he went. But one day he had a very important meeting so he left her behind with her mother. Her mother had left her in the garden with the gardeners and had gone inside to get some lunch. Once Elizabeth's mother had gone inside, the gardeners grabbed the screaming girl, stuffed her into their van and drove off.

When Mr Kent got back, he was devastated. He went back out and searched for his daughter but couldn't find her. A couple of years had gone by and still no news until one day …

Elizabeth was now thirteen years old and was a robber. She knew it was bad but she had to otherwise she wouldn't get any food.

One day while Mr Kent was out in the streets he realised someone was searching through his pockets, he turned around and saw a girl staring up at him, terrified, like a mouse to a cat. He thought he had seen her before, but still took her to court. When they were in the court room, they found out her details and told Mr Kent. She was Elizabeth Kent, his daughter. He was so ecstatic that he ran up to her, hugged her and cried. They then drove off together, hand in hand.

Asmaa Shah (13)
Islamia Girls' School

My Unfortunate Morning

I stood there like a rocket ready to blast, I was about to start my first day at St Mary's High School. My shocking hair was sticking out of all corners, as a Vandegraaff generator had just touched me. My grubby face was full of mucky, perfectly rounded spots. There was so much lose material in my top that if I wrapped that material four times, it still wouldn't be enough to wrap me another time. Even my school trousers were discoloured, only because my thunderous washing machine washed my mum's deep blue shalwar kamiz on delicates in lukewarm water. I looked like a state of horror.

Hoot-hoot. Ooh no, the school is here and nothing's right. I ran up the stairs, so fast the banisters started to shudder loudly; I thought the staircase was going to fall out of the stairs. When I got to my room I picked up the over-used wooden hairbrush and started brushing my excessive hair.

Hoot-hoot. I just grabbed my flimsy bag and ran downstairs and said bye to my mum, who sympathised with my hideous uniform. I climbed onto the bright yellow school bus, when my grandma came out in the multicoloured night suit and said that I had forgotten my mini teddy bear charm for luck, for my first day. I walked off like the Hunchback of Notre Dame. I galloped quickly onto the bus looking around at uninterested people for me to sit next to. There was a girl with thick oval glasses and she had a pile of books on her lap. I sat next to her throughout the bus' noisy, grubby sounds. When we arrived in school a very noisy parade greeted us.

Nabilah El-Harraj (13)
Islamia Girls' School

A Night In A Haunted Mansion

The ancient mansion had been perched above the hill as long as anybody could remember. It had once been the grandest and most prosperous in the village, but after the death of its very wealthy owner it had fallen apart. Ivy had snaked its way upwards and covered the crumbling walls like a skeleton's hand. Huge trees lent on the upper floor windows sheltering them from view.

One windy, menacing, frosty night a brave girl by the name of Sally decided to explore the mansion herself. The thin beam of light streaming from the torch she carried did not entirely reveal the mansion's grimy secrets. Cobwebs were draped on every available space. Creepy-crawlies had made their homes in antique wardrobes and stately paintings. Thick layers of dust had plastered themselves on the once crystal clear windows; wooden furniture once so luscious and well looked after had been left to rot.

Her heart beating twice as fast, Sally tentatively stepped over a pile of peeling books and avoided the remnants of a shattered chandelier. Somewhere an owl hooted in the darkness, a gust of whistling wind swept through the trees making them sway and shower the ground with leaves like confetti, and the sound of hundreds of flapping wings could be heard from above as owls and bats settled themselves for the night on the roof.

In the corner the door swung open slowly, the rusted hinges creaking all along. Sally looked up from the unnerving masks she was gawking at and gasped!

Ruba Ramadan (13)
Islamia Girls' School

A Monster In Your Cupboard Story

I woke one morning and felt hungry but I couldn't really move at that point in time because my human was still asleep. I waited for ages, but it wouldn't move. I threw my favourite can of deodorant at it, 'garbage after weeks' it jumped out and ran downstairs. Finally, I could get out and retrieve my deodorant, I had to hold my nose because of the nice smell and it was much too clean.

Well, I'll do that when I'm able to show myself around here. It was time so I went back into the cupboard and on my way back to the home of monsters-in-the-cupboards when I bumped into the tooth fairy. She was in a grumpy mood (must have gone to the wrong side of the pillow this morning) and got angry. I knocked her teeth out of her bag by accident so she whacked me round the head with her purse, I don't know what she carries in it, but it is hard!

I continued my journey back home when a big hole appeared in my path, it grew larger and larger, wider and wider and sucked up most of my teammates but for some reason I wasn't taken in. I stood and thought for a moment why I wasn't taken and then I put a burger in my mouth with a mould sandwich and tried to get up.

Asim Fiaz (13)
Normanhurst School

My Beloved

My beloved, you in my arms makes a tear drop from my eye. I have loved you all my life and now we are still as strong. We hug on the sofa like it's a normal part of life but when we first met I found it wonderful when we held hands. Has the spark gone from our relationship? Not at all, I love you just as much as I used to, I always have, always will. Till death us do part, we shall be together forever, or will we? Will our relationship fade? Will you bring tears to both of our eyes? I don't want that, I hope you don't. Every time I'm with you, my life feels complete. My stomach flies away in butterflies and my heart feels as light as a feather.

My love, I feel we are dying, not physically, but relationship wise. I feel we are having an argument, have you been avoiding me? I'm not sure, I feel like a lost puppy. I feel like you don't want to love me. You do, but you don't want to. I have always loved you and I will continue doing that. You are the one for me and I love you more than anything that I have loved. You are perfect in every way, how can I not love you?

Do you know? Do you know my secret? It wasn't meant to happen. I didn't mean for it to happen but that doesn't matter, we can get through anything, we can get through anything, can't we?

Joe Woodcock (13)
Normanhurst School

Love Never Dies

For once in his life he was going to do it! He was going to ask the love of his life out. He got it all planned and his words perfect for her. After work he looked in Vanessa's office for her, she was packing up her work quite quickly. She said, 'Oh hi Nick, sorry I'm in a bit of a hurry.' He asked for a few seconds with her when they were going down stairs to the drizzly main road. She agreed so he started to explain his feelings when she ran over and hugged another man, 'I've got to go Nick sorry.' She walked away with him and his heart.

The skies poured as well as his eyes and his heart. He felt broken, feeble and hopeless. He couldn't believe that his ideal, perfect woman had walked out of his life, he couldn't find a point in living anymore.

He lived his life pointlessly every day from then on, feeling upset and forgotten all the time. One day he looked up and saw his ex-beloved shouting at her new man. It was a big argument. Vanessa stormed off and like always Nick went over to her.

'Are you OK?' he said.

'I was stupid. I never should have been with him, it didn't feel right, I need you and I love you so much, I didn't realise it until now, we are perfect together.'

The next day Nick gave Vanessa twelve flowers, eleven real and one fake. He told her, 'I will love you until the last one dies.'

Hannah Fullilove (13)
Normanhurst School

The Legend Of King Tyras

Long ago in the kingdom of Khared, lived a great king named Tyras. He respected his many citizens and he helped them live happy and prosperous lives. He also listened attentively to the views of his people. One day his advisors told him about an infamous beast that tormented the people to the west of his empire.

The king led his army on an expedition to Haridas. They arrived in the town four days later to find an area controlled by a merciless king and his frightful beast. The king of Haridas was called Lathas and he treated his poor people like his very own personal slaves. The army of King Tyras reached the gigantic city walls and an army of soldiers came through the gates to fight the army of King Tyras. The king looked up and he saw the hideous monster, it had four murderous arms and four abnormal eyes, it reminded him of a wolf with its huge bloodthirsty teeth. The monstrous being came towards the brave king. He used his bow to fire arrows at the creature but these just bounced off one by one. King Tyras dropped his bow onto the floor; he got hold of his sword. The king swung his sword towards the monster aiming at his leg, he fell instantly to the ground and the king stood proud and, with a final show of power, swung the sword into the monster to show the beast was dead.

George Dew (12)
Normanhurst School

Hero

It was a very bright, sunny day in the town of Varrok and many people were out doing their daily things. One in particular was Archer Amo who was doing fletching by the general store when someone came to her with a problem; they needed her to get rid of an uninvited skeleton with her amazing range skills. Amo was confident so set off to slay the beast, and succeeded, then carried on with her daily routine.

Later that day another person approached Amo with another request to get rid of something unwanted, this time a dragon! Amo was a little less confident but loved a challenge so set off to slay it and again succeeded. Five times that day people requested Amo to rid unwanted visitors and every time she succeeded, against moss giants, vampires, wolves and bears. Amo found it strange because she wasn't normally asked this many times but she took it as nothing and carried on.

The next day she received a letter ordering her to go to the king's palace that day at 7pm. Amo couldn't think what it could be about. She entered and to her surprise she saw a hall full of her friends and colourful balloons. The king told her yesterday was a test of her bravery and she'd passed with flying colours and was to be named as the Mayoress of Varrok! She was so excited and enjoyed the rest of her day at the party.

Rebecca Sullivan (13)
Normanhurst School

A Day In The Life Of A Poltergeist

Those mortals never rest; they always run around after their so-called children. I can never come out of my hiding place without being seen by one of them whinging, screaming alien things. Last night I crept downstairs, managing not to squeak the wobbly step. I entered the grand sitting room, I saw lots of children sleeping on the floor and sofas and one was lying on the space where I normally like to sit. A few of these mortals had sweets covering their faces and kept on fidgeting. I crept over to the sofa trying not to disturb the sleeping. I picked up the first human being and placed her on the floor. I sat in my space and read the nearby magazine. I remember reading something about a girl called Paris something or other; the story explained that she might be pregnant. I really didn't think something like this was important but it was to these mortal girls.

Suddenly I felt a kick on my arm and I heard a sudden movement, the human being next to me was awake! Her face was paler than mine, paler than chalk, paler than paper, paler than anything that was white. She was shocked and headed away, she screamed. I heard footsteps running down the stairs. My life has just ended; mortals had seen me and looked me in the eye!

Charlotte Mulligan (13)
Normanhurst School

The Board

It was a stormy night and the friends were gathering for a sleepover. These friends often met for sleepovers but tonight was a different night, it was requested that one of the friends would smuggle an Ouija board. They were tempted to gain secret knowledge through realms of the occult.

They had dinner and brushed their teeth, they then naughtily ate sweets until the adults went to sleep. The children, knowing what they were doing was wrong but enjoying the suspense, lifted the cover off a box displaying Ouija Oracle. They were ignorant and thought it was a joke and lit black candles to encourage evil spirits to speak in the human realm. They asked if a spirit was present and the planchette started spinning at a great speed.

The planchette flew off the board and plummeted to the ground with a clang! A vapour-like mystical entity ascended from the board, it said, *'How dare you disrupt my peace!'* The children's skin became like a sick, cold touch had laid its hands upon it, although the house was quite warm. Then there was the crack of fork lightning as the children hastily tried to pack away the board. The children were scared stiff and could not sleep for the night, although they stayed silent in cold fear. What was the entity? Was the lightning the entity's wrath? It's up to you, just be sure to remember and think of this story anytime you go to a sleepover!

Oshien Sheedy (13)
Normanhurst School

The Devil's Disciple

I woke that fateful day in a cold sweat. The reason I awoke like this was because I had had a dream so terrible that I can't even write it down on paper, it terrified me out of my mind!

On that fateful day, it happened to be Friday; I was in class, Miss Calon's art class when the first strange thing happened. Kate, who sat at the back of the classroom, gave a scream. Everyone looked round, she had gone plum-purple and her eyes had gone black! In the end she was sent to the school nurse.

It was break and we were playing football. Kate walked onto the pitch, this was weird because she had never liked football, then I realised in her purple hands was a blood-stained gun. There were screams and shouts as metal slug after metal slug sank into my friends' bodies. Then, as I knew she would, she turned on me. I turned and started running. *Bang* was the last thing I heard before I woke up and the real nightmare began. I could just make out a purple face with black eyes, 'Hell-o,' it said.

Edward Harrison (13)
Normanhurst School

The Connaught Legend

In the middle of a dense forest lies a stretch of water called Connaught Waters. Families spend hours over there walking around the lake with their dogs but no one goes there after dark because of the legend. It is said that a monster lies beneath the lake and drags dogs from the edge of the water. The legend started over fifty years ago when over a period of time, dogs used to go missing after dark. A scientist heard of this and decided to investigate by putting a boat on the water with underwater cameras and ultrasound equipment. He spent a whole week on the lake day and night with his faithful bullmastiff called Buster. After a while he thought that there was nothing there and left Buster in charge on the boat while he went to a pub with his friends for a drink.

A couple of hours after the scientist had left the boat, bubbles started to appear around the boat and the water got very murky. Buster started to panic and howl very loudly because the boat was tipping over. Just as a huge black shadow started to appear, Buster decided to jump off the boat and swim for his life. He swam faster than ever before with the shadow chasing after him, he could see his master running around the edge of the lake calling and Buster just reached the edge before it caught him. Buster was safe but who will be next!

Ryan McDonnell (12)
Normanhurst School

Nature Turns Upside Down

There lived a tribe called Eniagis. They were peculiar people, unlike other tribes; they didn't eat meat or practise voodoo. They were peaceful and believed in kindness and equality, however, don't be fooled, their daily schedule was strict.

Tidy lump of soil
Visit flowers
Water forest
Collect vegetables
Cook tribal dinner
End day by offering praises to the sun.

The sun rose, the songbird sung and the schedule had begun. They tidied their soil but realised there was a problem …

'The soil's dry and crumbly, how can I spread it out evenly?' inquired a tribe member.

Confused but determined not to let it ruin their day, they ploughed on.

The morning was carnage:

Water that was usually collected throughout the night had fallen and dried into the land.

The wind was so strong that sweeping the huts was impossible.

The vegetables had been trodden on.

By midday it was so chaotic that an emergency meeting was held.

'The world's turned upside down, nature has been destroyed!' cried a hysterical member of the tribe.

'Stay calm, nature's our friend, we have to restore it,' advised an elder.

Without a moment's confrontation they began working. They split into groups, gathered water and found methods to reduce the wind's interference. By sun fall everything was calm, the Eniagis land had been restored. To this day they are optimistic and joke, 'At least we'll be prepared next time!'

Siobhan Wright (13)
Normanhurst School

The Pied Piper Of Hamelin

It was a midsummer's day. At the time I was nine. I was playing with my dad in the garden when I heard three beautiful notes being played by a man called the Pied Piper. He had a ripped black T-shirt, blue jeans and no shoes.

As I followed the music I saw all the children in the village following the man as well as me. He seemed to be taking us to a porthole. At the time I was in a trance. As I looked into the porthole I saw the largest house.

Then I looked further into the porthole and I saw around 70 acres of land. As all the children went into the house I heard voices screaming my name … it was my parents. I did not care, I just ignored them. It was my turn to go through the porthole. I started to dance because I was about to go to Heaven. For some reason I could not get through the porthole. It looked like I was too big to get through. The porthole started to close slowly as I started to sigh. My dream slowly faded away.

As I walked home I was so depressed that I rolled the whole way home seeing as I was so big. Because I did not listen to my parents when they were screaming at me to come down, I got no dinner for a week. I didn't care. All I knew was that all my friends were gone.

Neville Rivelino (11)
North Bridge House School

The Lizards Of Ocho Rios

A long time ago there was a town called Ocho Rios which means eight rivers, it had a problem. It was infested with lizards. They destroyed everything electrical. This annoyed the townsfolk.

They cold not sleep and were awoken by the nightly croaking. Their jobs suffered. One sunny day, A Rasta appeared on the mayor's doorstep and said, 'Ya might be needin' mi services mon.' The mayor was called Clinton Lewis and looked puzzled for a moment until something clicked inside his head. He remembered the lizards!

'Ooohhh! You may help with the red-striped lizards with purple spots. I hope you're the person we have been waiting for! What is your name, brave knight?' asked the mayor.

The mysterious Rasta raised his left brow quizzically but casually replied that his name was Jacob and explained that he should be ridding the Dali Lama's town of locusts, but would help the people of Ocho Rios first, which would only cost 600 US dollars.

Mayor Clinton Lewis screamed with excitement and said that he would pay US$600 if only Jacob would spare them from these dreadful lizards!

Jacob stepped into the street and whistled! There was a deep rumbling. The mayor could see five elephants with five Rasta men riding them. They took down five cases and opened them. The Rastas began to play improvisational jazz. The lizards jumped up, put on sunglasses and began to dance. They were last seen in a conga line heading for Negril.

Aodhan Buckley (11)
North Bridge House School

The Pied Piper Of Hamelin - The Aftermath

The wind blew the litter about the streets. Mayor Bill Brixton looked out of his office window dismally. It was 1 o'clock and Brixton was thinking about what his lunch would be.

This was typical of Brixton. Always thinking about food. But, being fair, he was having a very trying day. Since the children of the town had disappeared three days ago, he had had no peace. Whenever he left his office gangs of enraged parents would mob him and demand to know where their children were. The police were sick of keeping them back and the chief had resigned the day before.

Brixton lit a cigar and thought about the street musician who had started it all, who had taken the children away, and hadn't come back. Why hadn't he given him the money he'd promised him? All he wanted was £1,000. Was that too much to ask for freeing the town from the rats?

But, in a moment of stupidity Brixton had refused to keep his promise. Because Brixton had been thinking of his ego once again. As soon as the rats were gone, Brixton had planned to invite the party leader to the town, throw a party and get promoted to another post in the party hierarchy. Leaving the industrial slum the town was, forever.

Brixton had always thought that the musician was a mysterious man, from the moment he arrived in the town. Both his ears were pierced and he wore a dirty leather jacket, plaid trousers and a red beret. And that strange flute that hung around his neck, the flute which gave out such heavenly music that had charmed all the children. That man was a very mysterious person, more sinister than anyone Brixton had ever met, especially those flashing blue eyes.

His secretary came in, ending his train of thought.

'Sir,' she said, 'here is a petition from the council demanding your resignation.'

'What!' said Brixton, but his secretary had left. He thought a moment. *Should he resign?* He had resisted the idea before. *But why not?* Resigning would mean no more dreary meetings, no more in-trays stuffed full of unanswered correspondence. It would also mean no more six-figure salary; but it would give him some freedom, after two years of blame for the town's difficulties.

He made up his mind on the spot, signed the paper, put on his jacket, took his coat and grabbing his bag, walked to the door.

Oh freedom, freedom at last, he thought.

Louie Brockbank (11)
North Bridge House School

The Pied Piper Of Hamelin

Songtown was infested with folk singers. They made such a racket that at one point, the town council paid them to be silent! They weren't.

One day, a guitarist appeared. He walked into the town centre and asked the mayor if he wanted to lose the folk singers. He replied yes and the guitarist offered his services for a sponsorship deal with Coke.

He produced a guitar, played three notes and strolled away. As he went, folk singers appeared from everywhere to follow. He kept going until he was gone.

When the guitarist came back, the mayor got a reminder of the deal, for he had completely forgotten! 'Uh, oh …it'll be ready by … 3 o'clock! Absolutely, you will *definitely* get the contract! It's not like we … forgot or anything!'

They met at the town square and the guitarist received the contract. He hastily scanned the pages, line after line, until his eyes came to a stop. 'This is for Sprite. I said Coke. Pepsi at the least.'

'We're a poor town,' the major said, shoving his bulging wallet down his pocket. The guitarist produced a match. He struck it upon his teeth so fast that it caught fire. He burned the contract.

He stormed off, his grey pupils now a fiery-red. He pulled out his guitar and played once more. This time, pop stars, Madonna, KISS, everyone on 'American Idol' and all good musicians followed him as he advanced away. 'Mock Madonna' was the town's greatest tourist attraction!

Songtown was silent.

Joseph Sellars (11)
North Bridge House School

The Four Dragons

A long time ago, there were no rivers on the Earth, but only the Eastern Sea, in which lived four dragons: The Long Dragon, the Yellow Dragon, the Black Dragon and the Pearl Dragon.

One day, the four dragons flew from the sea into the sky, playing hide-and-seek in the clouds.

'Look!' the Pearl Dragon cried.

The other three dragons looked down to where Pearl Dragon pointed. On the earth, there are many people putting out fruit and cakes, they are begging God to send some rain, so their children could eat.

There had been no rain for a long time. The crops withered, the grass turned yellow and fields cracked under the scorching sun.

'People will die!' said the Yellow Dragon.

The Long Dragon nodded, 'Let's go and beg God for rain.'

Then they leapt into Heaven.

In Heaven, Long Dragon said, 'Please send some rain on the Earth, if you don't they will die.'

'Alright, you go back first; I'll send some rain down tomorrow,' God agreed, when he was watching people dance.

'Thanks, Your Majesty!' The four dragons returned happily.

But after several days there was not a drop of rain.

They didn't want people to die so they scooped the water from the sea and sprayed it towards the sky. The water dropped like rain and saved people. They did that even though they might die for doing so.

But God heard this and was unhappy about it. He killed the four dragons.

They changed into four rivers; Heilongyiang, Yellow River, Changjiang and Zhujiang.

David Zhu (11)
North Bridge House School

The Pied Piper Of Hamelin

Once, a long time ago, Pedestrian town was a paradise to vermin rodents. The mayor had no idea as to how to send the rodents out of the city leaving Pedestrian town rodent-free, but as I tell you it was not easy. The rodents raided cupboards, fridges and pantries for their vile hunger. They left diseases in the town. The mayor was struggling to help his city.

Then a very strange person strode in. He claimed his name was the Pied Piper and that he could send the rodents out of the city. The mayor offered him an appreciative amount of money, fifty guilders to be exact. But the Pied Piper wanted a thousand. The mayor agreed.

The Pied Piper entered the streets, pipe in hand. The Pied Piper played a sweet tune on his pipe that festooned the town and from nowhere rodents poured into the streets and followed the piper out of the town and into the river. Eventually the rodents drowned.

When the piper went to the mayor to collect his salary the mayor offered him fifty guilders. The Pied Piper was upset, he wanted the salary he was promised, but was unable to get what he deserved. The piper vowed to use the power of his pipe against the city. The mayor and his assistants did not take this seriously. The Pied Piper was furious and thought of a way to get the mayor back. He ended up taking all my friends away, I was not meant to go. After the children had left the town the mayor was devastated, he offered another amount of money but the piper could not trust the mayor and never brought my friends back. Then he vanished.

Some say he went with the children, but I don't know for sure I was left behind, to tell this story.

Clarence Adjei-Attah (12)
North Bridge House School

The Pied Piper Of Hamelin

One day we were all in town, my friends and I. We were walking along near the mayor's house and suddenly we all saw the mayor come out, we were so surprised. It was an amazing sight, we saw the mayor in real life. We said hello to him, but he ignored us and for some reason he acted like he wanted us gone for good.

The next day was a town hall meeting. Everybody came and the mayor said, 'I want all you rats out of this town!' Everybody was shocked about what the mayor had said.

The next day the Pied Piper came along to town and said to the mayor that he would get rid of the rats if they paid him and they accepted his offer.

Later on that day the Pied Piper took a pipe and began to blow in it and straight away all the rats and mice came and followed him. The Pied Piper took all of them to a river and all the rats fell and drowned, all except for me, at that time I was spying.

Later that day the Pied Piper came and asked the mayor where his money was. The mayor said that he wouldn't pay him. The Pied Piper was really angry and banged his fist on the table.

The next day he did the same thing as he did to the rats but with all the children, including the mayor's daughter. He took them to a cave and disappeared with them.

Shayan Mahinfar (12)
North Bridge House School

The Pied Piper Of Hamelin

Behind the huge thick doors which led into the cave, was a wonderful world in which fairies, mermaids and other creatures lived. It was full of love and warmth. Everyone who went there felt special. In that place there was no sadness or unhappiness. The children who followed into the cave after the beautiful and magical music, played on a pipe by a mysterious man, were amazed to see Lilia - that was the name of the unforgettable place.

Children forgot about their parents, friends and the real world as soon as they entered. It was like they never lived on Earth. Lilia was an amazing place but it also erased memory about your past. That's why none of the children would go back to try to find their way home. However, this was not the only scary thing about Lilia, most of the creatures once were innocent kids just like these were now. That's why if you have a little memory about the past you should run back, try not to listen to the pretty music of Lilia. Try to run, run, as far as you can.

I was told this story by one boy, he was captured by the mysterious man and had seen Lilia. He survived because he loved his mother so much that no magic could have erased her. That memory helped him remember the world and escape from Lilia. He saw what was happening to the other kids and he got frightened and shocked. He began to panic and shake. He closed his eyes and ran away.

'I am an old man now, but what happened to me that day I will never forget. It was the most wonderful nightmare!'

Those were the last words that he said to me.

Elizabeth Nenarokov (12)
North Bridge House School

The Pied Piper Of Hamelin

One dreary morning, a strange man strolled into town. He wore a a red and yellow coat (no fashion sense) and no matter how long I looked at him I couldn't place his birth or kin. Eventually he walked up to me and asked, 'Excuse me Madam but may I ask, which way it is to the town hall?' He spoke in a strangely high but calm voice.

'You may ask,' I replied. 'By the town hall, do you mean that flamboyant building over there?' I shook a wing in a roughly easterly direction and to my surprise he strode off in that direction.

Ten minutes maybe twenty passed and out into the market strode the man and the entire sweating council in tow. At his lips was a flute, but no sweet music came from the pipe, just three shrill notes. In the first second I thought nothing of it, in the second came a rumbling and in the third …

Rats - from every window, every door, every nook, every cranny, every tile, every gutter. Rats in every colour (well, not yellow, orange or blue, but I do think I saw a couple of pink ones and a purple and red one stalking along in the shadows), every shape, every age, who happily danced behind the prancing piper. As the party went from street to street, more and more rats joined in. Soon they were dancing out of the town and that was the last of those rats.

Eleanor Doman (11)
North Bridge House School

The Pied Piper Of Hamelin

It was a lovely summer's day and I was playing with a neighbour when this beautiful sweet music grasped our attention, as if an angel were calling us. We were immediately drawn to it.

When I heard the amazing music of a far-off wondrous land, I rushed outside and all the children were flooding out of their homes. We all started skipping joyfully to a mountain from where the sound was coming, I couldn't stop myself.

When I got closer, a door in the side of the mountain opened where all was happy and peaceful, calm and tranquil, where trees blossomed, flowers grew and all the little woodland animals were feeding and making nests. But just as it came into view I suddenly became completely out of breath, my legs had given up on me and I couldn't go on any further. My legs had turned into jelly, it was like someone had made it happen, by some sort of magic and I instantly fell to the ground.

Laying limp and lifeless on the grassy field, I called out to my friends for help, but my call was not answered, they didn't seem to hear me, they just skipped on contentedly not even blinking an eye at me struggling hopelessly. It was like they were in a trance.

My friends pranced to paradise, for their new beginning in the side of the mountain, as I lay contorted in the empty cornfields, cold and disappointed that I didn't make it, watching my friends get swallowed up by the mountain. I sobbed helplessly.

I guess it wasn't to be.

Amy-Jane Cotter (12)
North Bridge House School

The Pied Piper Of Hamelin

A couple of years ago this mysterious man took all the children, except one. We are not sure if the child was left for a purpose or the mysterious man did not know he existed.

The boy that was left had become a man. But every night he would wonder what would have happened if he had gone. People told stories about this extravagant place, but it never changed his perspective of the magical place.

The next day the boy's mother said, 'Why don't you follow your dreams?'

He really wanted to go so he ran up the stairs and packed his bags and set off. To be truthful he didn't know where he was going so used his instinct.

After days it felt like going around in circles like endless deserts. The problems started to occur when he nearly ran out of water, so he started to panic. He knew if he could see someone he would be saved.

After hours and hours he saw a person in the distance. So he cried, 'Help!'

The person ran and collected him. The boy in his last gasps said, 'Do you know where the children are?'

'I'm the Pied Piper, also in this place you never age.'

Suddenly the boy leapt up and was so excited. But the boy had to ask, 'Why did you leave me … ?'

Anthony Cox (12)
North Bridge House School

The Pied Piper Of Hamelin

It was a spring morning when it happened. I was waiting for my lunch when I had the strangest feeling. It was as if I were being drawn to one spot, but felt like I was flying. I had always wanted to fly but I imagined a lot of children do. The smell of a bakery with hot baking bread floated in the air as if it were a cloud. A rich odour of chocolate drifted in the breeze and I went into a state of deep relaxation, like when you wake up knowing it's a lazy Sunday morning.

I began to walk. It was as if the world rushed past. I went out of the house, down the front garden - the aroma of the flowers along the path I once loved had disappeared. I went across the street and came to the river. Hundreds of children had come too, they were also in a trance like me.

We were driven by natural child-like desires. Sitting on a log was a man. He had no facial hair with a red and yellow coat. He was playing a pipe, although instead of music, the wonderful sensations came out of the pipe. The man was telling us in a strange language of feeling that we wanted to jump into the river. Without a moment of hesitation I did and began to swim. I had always been on the fat side so I physically couldn't go any further. All the children swam on to go through a portal in the mountain. I stopped and desperately doggy-paddled back. I was lame. That was the fateful day. The day of the Pied Piper.

Aaron Fordwoh (11)
North Bridge House School

The Curse

A narrow sinister river runs down to a temptatious castle surrounded by sunlight. Forbidden to the Lady of Shalott. All she has to keep her company is a loom and a mystical mirror to show her the magic sights of the world outside. Day by day she sits at her loom, weaving the life she wishes to live.

And every night she hears a whisper cry, 'A curse is on you if you stay, to look down to Camelot.' And the whisper leaves her to yet another sleepless night. As she sits one day in the dark, cold room, a new image appears at her mirror, a tall, muscular man with a gorgeous face. He has women running after him yelling his name 'Sir Lancelot' he shakes his dark black curls behind his ears, rides off and disappears.

The Lady of Shalott falls instantaneously in love. She forgets the dark curse and with a flick of her long flowing dress she leaves her agonising life behind, but when she gazes back with a crack and a crash, the mirror splits in two. She realises with a frost in her toes, the curse has come upon her. She hurries and stumbles through the long grass and finds a sailing boat. With a hurried scribble she writes her name on the prow.

As she rides along the river, caved in by tall plants of barley and rye, the lady begins to sing a chilling song. Just as she nears Camelot she notices a sudden frost come over her. Within seconds the curse has ripped all life from her small, innocent, fragile body.

Lily Grant (12)
North Bridge House School

The Lady Of Shalott - Modernised

Once upon a time, in a city far away or New York for short, there was a young woman called Hillary Shalott. Hillary was an actress she had long brown hair, silk to the touch, brown eyes as brown as Fois Gräs.

She lived in the Sheraton Hotel overlooking the park. One day on her usual cruise to Abercrombie & Fitch, she received a phone call, it was her parents and they did not sound happy. They had received her credit card bills and had sentenced her to stay in her penthouse. Many days and nights passed and all she could do was look through her Venetian mirror and gaze at the life that she was missing. She could see all her friends, the city but couldn't touch any of it. She just wished that she could go out. The only people that knew that she was there were the hotel staff and her parents.

One day, while she was looking out of the window someone caught her eye. It was Johnny Depp-Lancelot. She fell madly in love with him at first sight but remembered that she was not allowed out of the penthouse. *What the heck,* she thought and ran downstairs to catch a cab to go to Broadway. On the way to the theatre a gunman drove up to the cab and shot her. When she arrived, the doorman opened the door only to see her lying dead on the seat.

Louis Merran (13)
North Bridge House School

The Lady Of Shalott

20th August

These four grey walls are making me depressed, I can't live like this. The surroundings are beautiful, emerald-green grass encircled by golden barley and rye. In front I have a tapestry, the tapestry of my dreams. I forbid myself to gaze through the window as I know about my curse, but when I stare at the mirror my longing for the outside world grows. I long for fun, laughter, love and companionship. I don't know when that will arrive but from now it seems like never.

21st August

Sunshine dances through my window as I wake at dawn; I decide to sing my mourning song deeply and lovingly as if to someone except no one seems to listen ... the reapers reaping early are savouring my voice.

Suddenly I glance at the mirror as I quietly end my song. Walking towards it, my heart fills with love at the sight of this man, Lancelot. His gorgeous blond locks dazzle in the wind, his ruby-red lips are sealed as he rides on a brown horse down to towered Camelot. I turn to the window as I can't take it anymore. Already the curse is coming upon me as the sky turns a horrid shade of grey and Camelot is in sight; but I have to see him, my only chance of life. As I open the door my dreams shatter into pieces. I'm not sure I'll reach him, I'm not sure I'll see him, but I'm sure I have to take the chance.

Jade De Robles Rossdale (13)
North Bridge House School

The Lady Of Shalott

It was dark and gloomy and the fair maiden was weaving away. It had been years, years in that tower. She wove and neither hope nor happiness came upon the face of the Lady of Shalott.

While weaving, the dark grey wind whirled round that castle, round and round those four grey walls and four grey towers. Conditions were hostile and depressing with small portions of food a day and guards as scary as a crocodile drooling over your head. There was no hope.

It was unfortunate that all the beauty lay outside while she had to remain in that grey ghastly horror. As dawn approached the sunrise was beautiful, and as the beauty swept the grass and flowers she started to weep. And as she did her eyes laid upon a very elegant looking horse running gracefully. 'Arrow!' Something had been calling it. And as it galloped a dashing knight appeared. And as she gazed upon the face of her heart's love he jumped on his horse and galloped away into the distance, though that great vision was soon damaged for he was heading for Camelot.

As tempting as it was to go to him, her courage always failed for passing through that tapestry was a path to death. Even if she did break through, Lancelot's heart was set on the queen. A rule violated, a friendship broken, Lancelot's heart was set. The Lady of Shalott grew impatient and as she got up she sliced the tapestry in half and set off to her heart's desire. As she ran thunder and lightning struck the ground and, as she fell into the boat, the sun started to set.

Gent Haxhiu (12)
North Bridge House School

The Lady Of Shalott

Every morning I wake up in the same grim colour of grey. I spend my time sewing tapestries, singing songs and sitting down to gaze at the beautiful surroundings around my castle on a little island.

One day, I was looking into my magic ball, gazing at the flowers and fields of barley when suddenly I came across the most handsome man I'd ever seen. He was on a large beautiful horse with armour, which reflected the sunshine. His hair was dark black and was pushed back in the wind as he trotted along.

He was so handsome that I left the magic ball and ran for the window to catch a last glimpse of him. Then I realised I was looking at Camelot where the man was trotting to. I then knew that the curse was upon me. The tapestry threw itself across the room, the mirror cracked and everything in the room was destroyed; so I thought I might as well go down to Camelot to see him.

I ran down the long spiral staircase until I came to the doors. I burst them open and found a small boat under a willow tree. I grabbed the boat and wrote 'The Lady Of Shalott' upon it. I climbed into the boat and set sail down the winding river to Camelot. The weather started to become stormy as I began to feel ill, but I was determined to see that handsome man again.

Jessica Kent (13)
North Bridge House School

The Lady Of Shalott - Modernised

It was Friday night. Lucy went out with her friends to central New York. Lucy was 18, she had a curfew, her dad John articulated clearly, 'I want you here by 11 o'clock, understand!'

She went out and had a magnificent time. It was already 1.45. Meanwhile at home John was looking at his watch every five minutes; he was phoning her mobile, but it was switched off. While Lucy was having a drink she fell on the floor. Her friends insisted that she went home. When she looked at her watch, it was past her curfew. Lucy knew that she was late but she didn't care because she was used to getting yelled at.

She finally arrived home. She opened the door and as she tried to sneak upstairs, the centre of the living room lit up. She heard a deep voice from the dark corner, 'Come here, now.' She followed the voice and stood in front of a shadow. The shadow stood up holding an electronic device. It was John. He started to shout fiercely, 'Where were you? Why are you so late?' She just stared at him with a foul look on her face.

John snatched her hand and dragged her to their truck! He drove off ferociously to a field. They got out and stood on a layer of stones. John pressed a button and a hand-held mechanism and a gigantic rocket appeared. John said to her miserably, 'You'll live here forever!'

Petros Poyiatgi (12)
North Bridge House School

A Short Tale About The Lady Of Shalott

Once upon a time there was a radiant young lady named Sarah Susie Shalott. She was a poor young girl who had been isolated in a broom cupboard by some heartless kids and the only way she could see out was from an old shoe. A few minutes later a hamster walked by and as soon as she even took the tiniest glimpse, she knew she had to have the hamster, Lancelot of Camden Town.

She could only escape by breaking and wrecking the door, but she knew if she did this, the kids would bully and beat her to death. She was so desperate for this hamster, she asserted herself that she would do this. Then suddenly she realised something … she had no way to break the door down. Except for an intermediate-sized piece of metal. The moment was so drastic, she tried everything. The door began to crack after a while and a hopeful grin grew upon Sarah-Suzie Shalott's face, but this smile was slightly overjoyed. Suddenly the door cracked open! Hope and love had taken over.

As soon as she set her sights outside the door karma had sprung and Shalott had been attacked by the yobs. They had stabbed her ruthlessly in the gut leaving her to die slowly and painfully. Bleeding and limping, she attempted to get to the love of her life, Lancelot the hamster. She was just about to approach him when she tragically fell down the stairs, hurt her back and died a painful death. As the hamster walked towards her he said, 'My name isn't Lancelot, but you are still pretty.'

Daniel McKeever (13)
North Bridge House School

The Lady Of Shalott

There was a girl called the Lady of Shalott. She lived in a castle surrounded by three other castles and four grey brick walls. She lived on an island where there were long fields of barley and of rye. There were large willows and lots of wild flowers surrounding the castle.

The Lady of Shalott longed to be out in that world, to have a boyfriend, to chill out having picnics with friends, admiring the flowers and their beautiful scents, but she could not because she had a curse upon her.

The Lady of Shalott sat in her room all day sewing her tapestry. She had a very dull and dreary life. In her room there were two special objects, a magical mirror that you could see outside with and a great big tapestry which she could sew her life on.

The Lady of Shalott looked out of her window and saw a handsome man called Lancelot, she fell in love straight away. Lancelot had slick, dark, black hair, always combed back and a very muscular body.

The Lady of Shalott fell in love straight away so she broke the curse. The tapestry flung itself across the room and her magical mirror broke from side to side. She ran down to the nearest boat and floated down to Camelot. The weather turned from sunny and unclouded to wet, cold and stormy. By the time the Lady of Shalott had reached Camelot she had died. Lancelot saw her and admired her beauty.

Philip Brown (12)
North Bridge House School

The Story Of Mary Shalott

Once upon a time there was a girl called Mary Shalott who lived on the opposite side of the M29 motorway. Every hour of her day she was surrounded by cars and lorries of all shapes and sizes. She lived amongst beautiful, shabby, barbed weeds and thorn bushes. However, her surrounds were not all bad. She had a lovely, rusty, sharp fence next to the motorway to protect her.

Beside the motorway there was an enormous tower block with the enchanting fragrance of Budweiser beer and Marlboro cigarettes. Inside this incredible building was a 16-year-old seamstress. Not even allowed to smoke yet, she owned her own business of sewing dresses and had an adorable 1-year-old child. She was a charming girl with a heart of gold and cuteness none could match. Unfortunately she could not go out in the open as she was too busy sewing dresses and seeing her life through Trisha (no, seriously seeing her life through).

But one day, sewing as she did, she saw through her window her old friend Lance Alot, a delightful boy who could woo any girl off their feet. However, he was going to run across the busy motorway. As soon as Mary saw this she turned off Trisha, threw her dress out of the window and rode her bicycle down to the motorway to save him. This would be her demise. When she was nearly beside Lance she collided with a speeding McDonald's truck and was immediately killed. Lance was devastated.

Lucas Greenwood (13)
North Bridge House School

The Lady Of Shalott

There once was a picturesque island and on this island there was a castle with four grey walls and four grey towers. In this castle lived a lass called Shalott. The lass' grandmother wanted her to rot and so she placed on her a curse, this curse meant that she'd need a hearse, but only if she saw Camelot.

This lass had a magic mirror from which she could see the world. One day she saw Sir Lancelot, although in the mirror he looked a dot. He sang 'Tirra Lirra'. She left the mirror and to the window she ran. She couldn't gaze at another man's face after seeing the knight in red. She cantered down the staircase to get a close up of his face. When she got there he had gone but still she could hear his song and so she looked up to the sky. That was the moment she knew she would die.

Camelot was what she had seen; the curse was on her, killed by need. Need it was to see the knight, a knight that made quite a sight. Despite the fact that her time had passed, she clambered up into a raft. A storm was brewing, the woods were waning, thanks to the curse it was now raining. In that raft she bit the dust. Sir Lancelot said, 'If I must.' He looked down and with good taste he remarked, 'What a quaint face.'

Max Burman (13)
North Bridge House School

The Lady Of Shalott

Dear Diary,

I am writing to you today to tell you about the vile life of being trapped in a grey castle with four grey walls and four grey towers. But to make it even worse, I have a curse and that curse is that if I look out of my window down to Camelot, I will die.

My daily routine is horribly boring. I can't look out of the window, so I look at the mirror and look at the fields of barley and rye and I see the reapers cutting their beloved crops. Around the tower lies a little river flowing down to Camelot. By the castle lies a dinghy which bobs up and down in the water. My only enjoyment is from the tapestry I sew. It has my memories and the moments that have happened to me since I have been in the tower.

I am locked up in a room knowing that if I break the curse I will escape in the dinghy down to Camelot. And then I saw him on his horse with long, thick, intense hair. That was it, I am out of here ... then it blew out of the window and broke into little bits, my tapestry was gone but so was I. I chased him all the way down the riverbank until he disappeared into thick shrubs. I was heartbroken.

Max Levene (12)
North Bridge House School

The Teen Of Shalott Road

It was a Monday, I hate Mondays, even if they are Bank Holidays. But that doesn't make any difference because I'm grounded. Anyway, my name is Melissa, I am fifteen years old and I live in east London.

I don't understand grounding, I mean, how is it going to help me? I didn't even do anything wrong! It's not my fault the train got delayed and I got home an hour and a half late!

Anyway, I was just sitting by my bedroom window drawing, when out of the corner of my eye I saw this gorgeous guy. He was flawless. He was heading towards the shopping centre. I got up as quick as a flash but then the fact that I was grounded slapped me round the face.

I sat there for about half an hour, contemplating the consequences of sneaking out but then I thought, *oh stuff it, what's the worst that can happen?*

Before I knew it, I was off down the road after him. I practically flew across the roads. Then it started to rain, I mean torrentially. I was getting drenched. Suddenly I saw him across the road. Without thinking I ran across. *Boom!* That's when it happened, I'd been hit by a lorry. The boy rushed up to my cold dead body and uttered these words, 'She is well buff innit.'

Painful. But Heaven isn't all that bad. Well, to be honest it's brilliant. Up here there's no such thing as grounding. Anyway, in about sixty or seventy years, my boy will be joining me.

Gus Mallett (12)
North Bridge House School

The Ghost Of Shalott

There are whispers in the trees, light struggling to beam through the brambles and thick, sinister, green foliage that was creeping up upon the unaware Lancelot.

He woke. Breakfast, commute, work, dinner, shower, bed, life was laborious and dull. Lancelot's prescient mind was highly imaginative, he was all too painfully aware of his failings.

Making matters worse, he owed a mortgage of £60,035 which encouraged him to turn to alcohol. Lancelot slumped on his woeful bed, where he shed tears for the regrettable choices he had made that had reinforced his boring depressing life - till now.

He slept. The ground beneath him seemed to give way and he fell into crusty black leaves. Lancelot pulled himself up from the debris and strolled along a verdant forest grove between two ancient weeping willows.

There, over the horizon were four walls and four grey towers, for some reason they appealed greatly and a wave of curiosity flooded Lancelot's mind. He travelled towards the ominous grey castle. Crossing a creaking unsettling bridge, through forbidding aspens and to the bolted menacing door. Up the cold spiral staircase adorned with beautiful tapestries. To the highest tower from where peaceful singing could be heard. There sat, with its back to Lancelot, the ghost of Shalott. Lancelot crept up behind the ghost, but it suddenly turned on Lancelot and a piercing painful screech attacked Lancelot's ears. The ghost flashed a knife and sliced and diced and Lancelot's lifeless body crumpled to the ground. Lancelot's ghost of Shalott brought to life by his imagination, became his deathly demise.

Oscar Dunbar (12)
North Bridge House School

The Lady Of Shalott

Once upon a time, on an island not far from Camelot, amidst the beautiful English countryside was a castle. On either side of the river were fields of barley and rye, where lilies delicately fluttered in the refreshing summer breeze. In this peaceful setting, however, was an intimidating castle, with four towers and four walls. Inside this castle lived the Lady of Shalott, a woman cursed to stay inside the castle. Night and day she's inside the small room of her tower, weaving what she saw in her mirror, a mirror that displayed to her the outside world as, was she to look out of her window, a curse would descend upon her.

Sometimes a group of elaborately dressed damsels would pass her tower, sometimes a shepherd boy would amble past her abode. But none of the passers-by would make a big impression on her.

It was a cool summer's morning. The sun's rays reflected on the dewy succulent grass. The day began as normal for the Lady of Shalott and she set herself about weaving the images she saw in her mirror. A bow-shot from her tower rode Sir Lancelot. Sir Lancelot was courageous, he was trotting through the serene barley fields on a horse with a bridle decorated with exquisite gems. He was dressed in armour, that reflected the sun's rays to create a brilliant light. It was said that any woman who looked at Sir Lancelot fell in love with him. The Lady of Shalott was no different. She saw him in the mirror, ran across to the window to see him and she felt a chilling sensation. She cried, 'The curse has come upon me!'

Kia Golsorkhi-Ainslie (13)
North Bridge House School

The Girl In The Mirror

I looked in the mirror, I saw something rather odd, a different coloured hair on my head. I plucked it out feeling no pain to find it was grey. I stared at this one hair for the best part of ten minutes. I then quickly ran to the shower knowing what I had to do. I grabbed the necessary products, cleaned the bottles twice before applying to my scalp. I used the hair dye three times consecutively. I then cleaned the shower four times before going to the living room.

The phone rang. I walked past it paying no attention to the rather eccentric tone and stared out the window. I stared at him. When looking at him, I was in a different world. The still ringing phone switched to the answer phone. 'Hello, it's Suzie Shalott leave a message.' Still paying no attention to the phone, I saw him go off for his morning shower, subconsciously I assumed my position in front of the mirror. Thinking about the grey hair and what it reflected? My age? Was it time I maybe left the house? A voice boomed out of the answer phone. I glanced at the window, he had left the house. I strolled over to the window in a routine-like manner, but what I saw next made me cringe. In that instant my whole life came crashing down. He was with someone. I watched as they kissed, talked and entered his sky-blue Ford Mondeo. I ignored everything I believed in and left the house, I ran across the road after him. He reversed. *Bang! Thud!*

Omar El Gazzar (13)
North Bridge House School

The Oxygen In Shalott

I am a 40-year-old woman who is allergic to oxygen. I know it is strange but it is true. It is now 2011.

My name is Sara and I live in Shalott Metropolis. In my house I have no windows as they let in oxygen, but I have a small room with a special mask that doesn't let in oxygen for a minute or two.

I don't know whether anyone knows that I'm here though, but I sing every morning, so I'm sure someone hears me, probably just the early postman.

One day when I was looking out of my special window I saw a tall handsome man with a glint in his eye and a shine on his teeth. This man stunned me with his boldness and courage. Then I suddenly realised that my minute had been up a few seconds ago. I screamed, but not with fright, with happiness. I was happy that I was free; even though my time was coming, I knew I was free.

I immediately ran out of the house screaming. People on the street kept on staring at me, but it didn't matter. I breathed in the air; it was strange. I could feel it killing me inside, eating my lungs.

I saw the 'man'. I ran as fast as I could towards him. I could feel my body being eaten up. I screamed at him, 'What's your name?'

Just before I died I heard him say, 'My name, pretty girl, is …'

Then I died.

Henry Buck (13)
North Bridge House School

My Diary Entry

Dear Diary,

This morning I looked outside and I saw the barley and the rye lying outside on the field. The lilies were blowing and I could see the magnificent many towers of Camelot. Starting through the many ages of my life I am drawn to this as if under a spell. The cold mornings make me shiver. I long to be on the river so I can flow down to my beloved Sir Lancelot. My deepest desire is to be with him. I've dreamed for this since I was a young girl, although my life has just begun. And although my love will go unsung, my greatest desire is to meet him alive, away from the wretched curse that's been laid upon me. Take me away from this hell, which I am forced to live. Please God, help me to get rid of this curse it's also keeping me away from my love. I have to go upon the boat and through the branches into the valley of the death and I imagine him to be on his knees holding a bright red rose and the sentence he exclaims is, 'My dear Shalott, I have desired this all my life.'

Gliding down to the tower ... birds and angels are around us singing and both of us holding each other tightly. Sir Lancelet glancing back at me with his sensational smile.

Diary, I will be away for a while to meet my love, but I'm not sure I will be back.

Fabiola Maddalena (12)
North Bridge House School

Captain Gabriel

In the 41st Millennium, robots called Space Marines are protecting humanity. Millions of humans are trained to become the Imperial Guard. The traitorous Chaos, Orks, Eldar, Tau, Necrons and Tyranids are invading planets under human control. However, this was just a game. How did this happen … ?

Shalott was playing Warhammer 40000 with her friends. She had brought a doll to characterise a woman in a cage. Suddenly, the doll's eyes started to glow red. She touched it and found herself here. In the middle of everything. She was the doll. She had to find Captain Gabriel. She knew what he looked like. However, there was also a curse. If she were ever to abandon the cage, her head would turn into a coconut! Nevertheless, she had to because that was the only way home.

Therefore, with new courage she left the lockless cage and ran for it. She found a heavy weapon team and asked them if they had seen Gabriel. 'I believe that he is at … 2 hours 30 minutes 4 seconds NNE,' the captain blurted. 'By the mall,' he pointed to a huge crumbling slab of concrete.

By every passing minute, Shalott was getting worried about the curse. At last, she found Gabriel fighting off Tyranids, but alas, it was too late. Even the aliens looked away in disgust. Gabriel stumbled backwards. 'Argh, your head,' he whined. Everyone started screaming and fleeing in all directions. Suddenly, the whole world went black then white and she was back at home with her friends playing Warhammer.

Batuhan Koc (13)
North Bridge House School

The Lady Of Shalott

There was once a lady, the Lady of Shalott. She would sit in her grim derelict castle with nothing but a mirror and a loom. All she had to do all day was sit at her mirror and see all the happy people outside. Then she would put them into her tapestry, because if she dared look directly through her window, a terrible curse would come upon her and kill her. She would also die if she left the castle.

One fateful day, she was looking into her mirror and she saw a bold red-crossed knight of the name Sir Lancelot. She instantly fell in love. Without a thought, she rushed from the cursed castle and leapt into a boat. Instantly the sky turned grey and thunder struck. Then it struck again! Suddenly she realised and she screamed, 'The curse has come upon me.' She knew from then she must pursue her love.

She pushed off from the side of the river and started to float down to Camelot. She sensed the end was near, so she sang her last song and died. The boat carried on floating down to Camelot.

The boat arrived at Camelot. Sir Lancelot was awoken suddenly by a scream. He walked to the window and peered out. There was a big huddle of people at the edge of the river. He rushed down and pushed his way through the crowd. He saw a young woman in a boat. He then bent down and said, 'She has a lovely face, may God lend her grace.'

Jordan Mehmet (13)
North Bridge House School

My Quest Begins

The juncture in time had come, the moment the curse that had served its purpose for so long had been broken. Now we were here as a consequence of the curse.

What demon, or which had laid such a trap for the Lady of Shalott? I (Sir Lancelot) and all the other Knights of the Round Table were waiting for the moment to come for the Lady of Shalott to be laid down to sleep in peace.

Suddenly everything went cold, so cold the branches around were freezing and wilting. Then the wind picked up causing panic. We all ran to the castle to seek refuge. Everyone was crowding at the door as though there was a force field there. I pushed to the front, what met me was crushing. There, laid the guards and all the people who were going to carry out the tomb.

There was a sudden howl in front of us, a little up the stairs. There in front was a monster, it resembled a wolf-like human. All the knights crowded round the front of the king in a line of barrier. The wolf ran towards the king. I ran towards the thing and I dug my sword in its arm and it whimpered and ran out of Camelot and away.

Later that night I was in the king's bedroom guarding when I saw it and heard its cry of revenge. My quest was about to begin.

Thomas Kershaw (13)
North Bridge House School

The Lady Of Shalott

There was once a lady named the Lady of Shalott. She lived in an old Victorian house which no one had ever heard of. Her grandmother had passed away a few years ago. She had brought her grandaughter up because her parents left the country when she was younger. Her grandmother had given her fortune to one of her acquaintants.

One day the Lady of Shalott came back from school and Suzan, her grandmother's companion, decided to lock the young lady in the basement and told her she would never see daylight again. The young girl tried her best to make any possible sound or gesture to be heard or seen, but failed.

The next morning she heard people outside her window having a discussion. She peered through her fractional window and standing in front of her was a young elegant gentleman. He had long golden hair and turquoise eyes. The Lady of Shalott instantly fell in love and didn't know how to depart from this locked-up damp basement. Suzan had people guarding the house, day and night, but she didn't care. All she longed for was to meet the love of her life. She picked up her bed and smashed it against the window. As soon as she reached out of her window she instantly got shot.

Lancelot came rushing towards her and was confused about what had happened. 'She is beautiful, why did I never have the chance to meet her?' he expressed broken-heartedly.

Jennifer Sulkin (13)
North Bridge House School

The Lady Of Shalott

Dear Diary,

I live on an island, surrounded by the river and long fields of barley, disassociated from the beautiful village, Camelot. I sit here, knowing a curse is on me while not knowing what it might be. Day and night, I sit here in this castle weaving, feeling lonely and despondent. Although I cannot see the outside world with my own naked eyes, I see it through the magic mirror where the shadows of the world emerge. I see the red-cloaked market girls and irritable peasants, sometimes even a shepherd lad or a training knight in crimson clad.

One day, I saw him through the crystal mirror, a bold knight riding between the barley sheaves, as the sunlight came splendidly through the leaves above. The armour he wore danced and clanked as he rode down to Camelot. His eyebrows glowed as the sunlight beamed; his charcoal curly hair capered and swayed loosely beneath his helmet. Down by the river he went, flashing his reflection in the pure and unpolluted water, singing a song, which melted away my heart.

I left the room and out the castle. I saw the water lilies, the helmet and the plume. The mirror cracked, 'half and half'. How terrified I became I knew the meaning of this; the curse had come upon me. But I did not hesitate. I found a boat floating alone. I wrote my name in front of it, loosened the chain and let the water carry me, down to Camelot.

Shi Shi (13)
North Bridge House School

Concerning Shalott

Some days ago a boat drifted into Camelot. In it lay a lady, clothed all in white. Around the prow was written 'The Lady of Shalott'. She was dead although no wound was visible and the physicians said she had not died of natural causes. I was intrigued and decided to explore this mystery. Hearing of an island of Shalott I took a boat up-river.

One the way I saw a large tapestry caught on a tree root. Collecting it I beheld the words 'The Lady of Shalott' inscribed across the top. Below was a detailed history of the kingdom for the last hundred years.

Landing at Shalott, I perceived a tower hidden among the foliage. Upon approaching I discovered a wild garden and in the tower a room with a bed and furniture. On the floor lay a mirror, shattered into pieces. As my fingertips made contact with the shards I heard the sound of breaking glass and a piercing scream. Flinging myself backwards the sound abruptly ended.

Crossing to the bank I walked to the nearest village. Questions regarding the island were met with distrustful glares until I found a young farmhand who talked of the fairy of Shalott, a fairy who lived on the island and sang sweet songs at dawn and dusk.

I returned then to Camelot to pen my account of these happenings. I hope some day to piece together all the clues, but am currently unable to do so and it nags at my mind.

Joe Faulkner (13)
North Bridge House School

The Lady Of Shalott

Once upon a time, when castles and majestic knights were still present the Lady of Shalott was singing a dulcet song in her lofty tower. It echoed across the vast barley fields and spacious flower beds, which River Eddy cut through, flowing down to the castle in Camelot. Unfortunately, not everything was as it looked. This was because there was a deadly curse on the Lady of Shalott which would be revealed if she dared to abandon the tower.

One splendid day when the sun shone vividly, a handsome red-crossed knight called Lancelot came riding by. His armour gleamed like the moon in a coal-black night. His pitch-black hair waved like silk in the wind. He rode and rode until he disappeared on the sinuous road to Camelot.

She left her wooden loom and paced two steps to and fro. She ran outside the tower and crawled into a slender boat on which she inscribed her name. There she floated on the curvy river, passing the birds that whistled calmly, when she began to sing a song - her last song. She sang it softly and coldly until her heart came to a sudden halt.

The boat tardily floated into Camelot where it came to a stop. Out came the villagers, men and women, knights and warriors. They all gathered around the boat with the body and stood there silently. Finally Sir Lancelot came to the front and articulated, 'What a lovely girl, may she rest in peace, the Lady of Shalott.'

Oskar Piotrowicz (13)
North Bridge House School

The Lady Of Shalott

There once was a lady named the Lady of Shalott. She was put in a grim gruesome tower and if she left the tower, the ghost of yesteryear would torture her until the day she died. She was sentenced because she decimated the ghost of yesteryear when she was human.

But one fierce night brave Sir Lancelot was strolling by. 'Off to slay a dragon,' he cried. She fell in love with handsome Sir Lancelot, so she left the web, she left the loom, she made three paces through the room, saw the ghost asleep and ran away as fast as she could. The Lady of Shalott jumped into a boat and immediately the sky went grey, thunder bellowed, lightning crashed and flashed and *snap* - her boat split in two. So she swam down to Camelot where brave Sir Lancelot was heading, but the ghost of yesteryear caught up with her. As she was diving down heading for the Lady of Shalott, the ghost of yesteryear dug a knife right through the Lady of Shalott's heart. Blood was pouring everywhere, the Lady of Shalott burst into tears saying, 'Oh Sir Lancelot, will we ever meet?'

Bold Sir Lancelot hearing this cry turned his horse around and rode to find the person who made it. Lancelot riding on his horse found the Lady of Shalott dead saying to himself, 'This Lady of Shalott looked like a kind and lovely person. Too bad I could not have met her.'

Angus Whitfield (12)
North Bridge House School

The Lady Of Shalott

Once upon a time, there was a beautiful lady who was named Shalott. She lived in a skyscraper by herself in the countryside. Below the skyscraper there were flowers, willows, aspens, fields and a river around. The Lady of Shalott was cursed, it warned her not to look through the window or the mirror would crack from side to side and she would die. But she did not know it. The Lady of Shalott often sat next to the mirror singing, weaving and watching what had happened in the world from her magic mirror and the people who lived nearby knew her by hearing her songs.

One day, when she was watching what had happened in the world, she saw a handsome man pass in front of her skyscraper. The man was very versatile, he looked like Beckham, his Kung fu was as good as Jackie Chan, his song was as wonderful as Robbie Williams and his name was Lancelot. As soon as the Lady of Shalott had seen him, she'd fallen in love with him. She rushed to the window and saw him.

Bong! The curse had come, the mirror cracked from side to side, the skyscraper began to break down and the Lady of Shalott ran out of the skyscraper, came to a bus station where Lancelot had departed on a bus. The Lady of Shalott also went on a bus ready to catch up with Lancelot. But *pang!* the bus exploded.

Laura Chen (13)
North Bridge House School

The Unwanted Surprise

The art gallery was silent. Every now and then I heard a woman's high heel chink against the floor.

I coughed and the silence made everyone turn. Someone mentioned my name. How did she know it? Suddenly half the crowd gathered around me, pushing and shoving to catch a sight of me and mumbling under their breath. One man asked for my autograph and then everyone followed. I tried to tell them they had the wrong girl!

The next morning my memory of the night before was completely erased. I had a dreadful headache! I only had a slight recollection of someone shouting to me in the art gallery. He said, 'Gee missy, you're gorgeous. Fancy something?' That was all. I could not remember anything else.

I laughed at the fact that someone considered me gorgeous. I laughed until my body started to ache. I came back to my flat and picked up the evening newspaper. However, this time the picture on the front page was of me! The headline read, 'A frog? No they're too pretty'. I carried on reading, my heart sank. It was all about my appearance and everyone was expecting a stunning lady, but instead they had me!

I dragged myself to the kitchen and to my excitement I had a message. I did not recognise the sender's name but I read it anyway. 'My darling! Gee, you still have not called me. A rose? No, you're too pretty! Fancy lunch?'

Gloria Good (13)
Queens College

Ms Beutchur

There once lived a woman, who was cruel, strict and fastidious. She was tall with black hair tied up in a tight bun, pursed lips and a pointy nose that was always held high. She wore a tight navy-blue skirt suit every day with black not very high-heeled shoes. She was the headmistress of Heathington School for Girls. Her name was Ms Beutchur.

She had a walking stick which she took with her everywhere, but never used. When she got to a door she started using it so that someone would open the door for her. If no one opened it she would wait. She had spies who knew everything about everyone and for reporting back to her were given privileges. These spies found out what pupils were doing at the weekend, if Ms Beutchur didn't approve she would see to it that they were grounded! If a pupil did something slightly wrong; got below a C in any piece of work; was one minute late for school; wore her uniform incorrectly or just a tad askew she would be suspended or expelled.

Every year the number of students became fewer and fewer because so many were being expelled because of this tedious tyrant of a headmistress. The school board realised this and Ms Beutchur was fired. A new headmistress was hired, she was poised, witty and polite, Ms Connell. Heathington school for girls was never better and the students were flooding in. As for Ms Beutchur she was never seen or heard of again.

Georgina Robertson (13)
Queens College

John And The Tide Boy

John wasn't sure what to do, he was standing in the salty water with his wellington boots. He could see the little island getting smaller every second, the island wasn't sinking but the high tide was rising.

On the disappearing island there was a little boy unaware of the danger he was in. John had already tried shouting at him, 'There's a high tide, come back while you can.' He guessed the boy was foreign since he was staring with questioning eyes. It was time for action; he walked on until the water could nearly get in his boots then he stopped. The water was too high so he ran back to the beach, took his boots off and ran towards the boy. Halfway he fell down in a hole and got himself wet. Now he was furious, he couldn't take anymore of this holiday. But as soon as he got on his feet again he saw an enormous wave approaching the island. All he had seen was the boy running and falling and then John was buried by water. Now he was with his back to the wet sand when he opened his eyes he saw the grey sky then he remembered everything and looked, on his side there was a body, the boy. He took his hand and felt the cold skin, John knew the boy was dead and that he had failed his task.

Bianca Mazzi (12)
Queens College

Lunch

Snug. Warm. Dark. Lovely living conditions for me. Enclosed in my small world I am content. Soft mountainous pillows envelop me.

Suddenly, light pours in, hurting my eyes. I look up and see a monstrous giant smiling down at me. Its vast teeth dripping saliva. It's as if I'm seeing my own death. Revolting eyes, gleam menacingly, four times my own size.

I dash and hide behind my brown bed. I blink, my mind must be playing tricks on me. But no, there are millions of spiders mirroring my every move. Some big, some small, some fat, some thin. Weird mutant life. What are these distortions? I stand still, terribly confused. All the spiders copy. I steal forwards. I look at a spider. It stares back. It doesn't appear very well. I feel sorry for this poor dishevelled creature. Then with horror I realise these are me. I'm looking at myself in some sort of wrinkled mirror, each groove showing a different version of me. I just want to get out of here.

Before I can move a gigantic hand scoops me up. A thick mass of what only this morning was my bed, quickly becomes my grave. As I live the last moments of my life, I think about my cobwebs, my luscious silk, but mainly of my family. The mouthful creeps into his stomach and all stops.

'Yuck! My sandwich tastes weird,' exclaims Pete, examining his bread unwrapped in crumpled silver foil.

Zoë Halpern (12)
Queens College

A Painful Birthday

I woke up on my eighth birthday, my family staring into my sleepy eyes. My mum and dad went into the kitchen to get my present, but they did not come back for ten minutes! I was getting a little bit worried. So my brothers and sisters and I decided to go into the kitchen and see what the matter was. I saw my mum and dad sitting on the kitchen table with the radio by their ear.

'What is the matter?' I enquired.

'Go into your room, pack your bags and meet me in the kitchen in one minute! Do you understand?'

Yes,' I said. I grabbed my brothers and sisters and ushered them into their room and told them to pack their belongings. Suddenly I heard a scream coming from the kitchen.

'Wait in here,' I whispered to my shaking siblings. I walked quietly into the kitchen, looking round every corner.

I entered the kitchen to find my mum and dad being tortured by a Hutu soldier. I begged him to stop it, but he threatened to kill me next.

'Take your siblings! Leave Africa, run Ababa run!' my mother squealed with pan … I could not let my siblings suffer like that, so I ran. I never saw my parents after my eighth birthday.

It has been thirteen years since my parents and another 800,000 people died in the terrible massacre between the Hutus and the Tutsis in Rwanda. My parents were Tutsis, that makes me one.

Georgia Knight (13)
Queens College

Elaine And Elvis

Elaine is a nursery school teacher at Battersea Nursery School. Elaine had always wanted a baby of her own. She and her husband Cliff had tried significantly and were just about to give up as Elaine was forty-six years of age. But then she found out about egg donation and she applied immediately at the Lister Hospital in London and she was thrilled.

After a few years on the waiting list, she had completely forgotten about it. But after the long wait she was given an egg! The two-week wait after she had had it was very worrying. Then came the exciting news that she was pregnant.

After a wonderful and busy pregnancy baby Elvis had arrived. Elaine and Cliff and the family were so thrilled and happy that everyone they knew went to visit them in the hospital. Elaine was the most happy, upbeat and calm person and mother in the whole of the Westminster and Chelsea Hospital. Elvis was so loved by everyone, he was a really special little baby.

When baby Elvis and Elaine were back home they had a big party and went everywhere. Elaine took Elvis to Harrod's, Claridges, Madame Tussard's, Oxford Street, Regent's Street, Kings Road, Sloan Square, Duke of York's and loads more places like Brighton, Cannes, south of France, Iceland, Finland, Greece and Ibiza! So he was a very well-travelled and happy baby at only nine months old.

Millie Dean (12)
Queens College

The Diary

All my friends laughed when I told them, they told me that my life was not interesting enough to write about in a diary.

It all started a week ago. It was a horrible day, cold and foggy. I was walking home from school, but I could hardly see a thing through the fog. Before I knew it I was lost. After a while, I found myself in a maze of twisting alleyways and cobbled roads. Then, through the fog, I saw a light coming from a shop window. It was the strangest shop I had ever seen. It seemed to be some kind of ancient curiosity shop.

Inside, I was greeted by a man who was very old and was wearing a Victorian suit. He stood, watching me look around. I saw the diary, bound in old leather and was strangely drawn to buy it, but I had forgotten my purse! Before I spoke he said, 'That's alright next time we meet you can pay me then.' I thanked him and as I left, the fog had suddenly disappeared as had the shop.

From that day on my life changed. For I found that anything written in the diary became true. What fun I had when my swimming teacher, who always put me in the learners' class, was fired when it was found that she couldn't swim and every essay I wrote resulted in an A Star. That diary was the best buy I ever made.

Sophie Woodall (13)
Queens College

The Bad Pizza

'Poppy, I'm going with Luke to get your pizza, do you want the usual?'

'Mum, can't I come, you always take me, what's wrong?'

'Nothing, Luke just wanted me and him to go this week, that's all; we'll be back in about half an hour.'

Poppy sat on the sofa confused; she heard the door squeak shut and the car door to her mum's VW slam shut. Luke was in the front driving. Luke was Mum's new boyfriend. He was strange and Poppy didn't like him. He always wore the same thing, so Poppy thought; ripped jeans, a T-shirt and cap. It never changed.

About an hour later when Poppy finished her homework, she called out, but no one was home. It was seven and Mum left at six. Poppy went over to the sofa and tried to turn on MTV; of course, the ancient TV didn't turn on so Poppy kicked it as hard as she could and then the news appeared, not MTV like Poppy wanted. As she slumped onto the sofa and looked harder at the tiny cracked screen she knew what had happened. Then a lady spoke.

'A tragedy has occurred at Al's Pizza,' she paused,' a young couple of about thirty were driving out of control when …' Poppy couldn't listen. She knew what had happened. Her mum was dead. Luke must have been drunk and crashed into Al's, the little VW was probably a blue stone, all smashed and dented. Poppy was alone.

Lucy Ellerton (13)
Queens College

The Sunglasses

Jemma flicked her long glossy hair. 'I got an A*,' was the first thing she'd said while hanging her coat up. And she was wearing the hair band I wanted. I felt the irritation rising in me and it wasn't even break time.

Of course she was the first to hand in her history project, managing to tell Mr Hastings how much she had loved doing it. She had slithered in to hold the heavy door for Mrs Silgid as well as complimenting Mary the canteen lady on the 'delicious' bagels. Everyone loved Jemma.

But I would show her up.

One minute they were beside me; the next minute gone! I would never have been able to afford them myself, but my ticket was chosen! 'Pink, 161,' I'd won the raffle! Dior sunglasses, probably donated by a lady from one of those double-fronted white houses in Notting Hill. Jemma had taken them and I was going to get them back.

I followed her into the bathroom, my shoes smacking the black tiles. The showdown would be dramatic! I could hear the banter of the girls in the cubicles; they would witness it! Her petite figure facing the mirror, I chose my moment; words ready to deliver like a razor, 'Give me my glasses!'

But as I moved closer, I saw myself in the mirror and the glasses. On my forehead.

'Are you OK, Rudi?'

'Yes Jemma.'

I felt guilty and I knew that I was in the wrong.

Rudi Salmon (13)
Queens College

The Concert

'Here we are!' Mum said eagerly. She parked the car in a small space outside the school and gave me my lunch in a brown paper bag, along with a kiss goodbye. I jumped out of the car and waved while I watched her drive into the distance. I walked towards the school, missing the front door, making my way round to the back where I met my friend Alice.

'You ready?' she said.

I nodded, 'OK, let's go.'

We waited for the train to come; Alice and I were always getting up to things, but never something like this. I sat fiddling with my thumbs, watching Alice dancing to her Walkman, but the loud sound of the train approaching got her attention. Alice and I have always been big fans of 'The Pink Roses'.

We were stepping onto the train when someone caught my eye. She had a newspaper in front of her face but I could still recognise her hair and I felt as if I had seen those clothes before. All of a sudden the papers dropped from her face and to my disgrace, my headmistress was standing before us. I then felt a cold hand on my shoulder and a loud voice spitting into my ear saying, 'You're in big trouble young lady!'

From that moment I knew I was not going to see The Pink Roses … ever.

Sophie Shalson (13)
Queens College

Music And Flashing Lights

Music and flashing lights filled the living room as I stepped in. Charity and I made our way to the back of the room to talk to a group of friends. About half an hour later, more people were arriving, older and younger. The living room was packed. So packed, Charity and I made our way to the kitchen to get ourselves a drink. After making small talk to a few girls and boys we hardly knew we decided to go and dance for a bit since quite a few people were coming out for some fresh air.

We danced for what seemed like hours in the dim light of the living room. We both had to sit down as our feet were aching. We started chatting to a few boys that were sitting next to us on the sofa. Everything was calm until we all heard smashing glass, a scream, a thud on the floor. Everyone fell silent. All you could hear was the music playing in the background and sirens sounding.

It all happened so fast, an ambulance came and men entered the room with an empty stretcher then out they came with a teenager lying on it covered in blood-soaked bandages wrapped around his body. The police were going round to everyone, questioning them. When they came to me I was so shocked I could hardly speak. After I had got over the shock of it all I called my mum and she picked me up straight away. That night I couldn't sleep at all, all I could hear were the sirens and people screaming. It could have been me.

Maya Parmar-Jenkins (12)
Queens College

The Haunting

Kate Mulberry was an only child; her parents had died in a car accident when she was eight. Since then she lived with a foster family, the Wellingtons. They had no children of their own, in fact they hated children. They neglected Kate and made her do everything around the house. Kate wanted desperately to have a new foster family. She knew they had only fostered her for the large sum of money her parents left her.

They lived in a large sombre house. Even though it had plenty of rooms, they made Kate sleep in the spooky forgotten attic.

One night, Kate woke to the sound of a woman's voice singing. She recognised the song … her mother used to sing it to her. She sat up and faced the moonlit wall; she could see the silhouettes from the trees outside against it. The windowpanes rattled in the whistling wind and Kate could see the lamplight from downstairs peering through the gap under the door. She sat there for a while listening, wondering whether to go downstairs.

Meanwhile Mr and Mrs Wellington had gone downstairs to investigate. When they turned the lights on, all the bulbs fused and a pale white figure edged towards them. After a while, the noise stopped and Kate went back to sleep.

The next morning she found the Wellingtons outside her door looking anxious.

'What's the matter?' asked Katie. 'You look like you've seen a ghost.'

'You're moving families, pack your bags and let's go,' ordered Mrs Wellington.

Rebecca Schlesinger (14)
Queens College

Revenge

The trees pushed past the car, shadowing over us like big green giants. It looked like someone was unravelling a big black sheet in the lonesome sky. I felt at any second we would get sucked into it like a vortex. After a couple of minutes we soon reached the house. The moment when I first saw the house, I began to shake. To me it was like a mansion.

When we went inside, my dad found some keys on the table and a letter saying that the west wing was forbidden. Even though this place scared me, I couldn't help myself. I grabbed the keys from the shelf and ran, making sure I could not be heard. It was really dark, I could hardly breathe from all the dust. I wanted to go back until I saw a seam of light coming out from under one of the doors. I opened the door slowly and walked in.

The room was covered with sheets, all over the furniture. I felt something drop on me so I quickly turned around and felt my shoulder. It was dark red. My heart was beating fast. I looked up and saw a dead corpse hanging from the ceiling.

Shocked, I turned around to see a lady all in white. She said to me, 'Revenge is sweet.' Straight away I ran to my parents screaming so loudly.

Then my parents did not believe me but now do they believe me? Revenge is sweet.

Sema Naqi (13)
Queens College

The Deserted Mansion

As I took my first step into the deserted grand mansion, a lizard slithered across the dark mahogany floor. I dusted the cobwebs out of my face and tiptoed towards the staircase. I lay my shoe down on the blood-red carpet of the creaking steps. The varnish on the banister was disguised by fluffy grey dust.

Upstairs was no different. I entered one bedroom, covered in dust and cobwebs. There, hung deep red curtains and a thick layer of red paint on the walls. A white dressing table was situated on one side of the curtains and an unpolished mirror to go with it. I breathed in a suffocating odour, which I coughed out instantly after. I walked over to the light switch and turned it on. There was only a single light bulb in the centre of the ceiling. The paper was peeling and it had turned yellow over time.

I turned around, my back to the curtains, facing the ghost-like dressing table, imagining a woman in white brushing her long black hair, staring motionlessly at the mirror. I gasped in fear as a preternatural figure approached me. It was the woman I imagined! She slowly limped over to me, one bony, ghastly, white hand in front of her. She rested it on my shoulder. Tears poured out of my eyes and screams escaped from my mouth. Her eyes were bloodshot with fury, flaming. I tried brushing the skeleton hand off but it wouldn't move and neither could I.

Hema Kathrecha (14)
Queens College

Nothing Is As It Seems

It was a dark, gloomy evening when Lisa arrived at her holiday house. She had booked it months in advance and was really looking forward to it, but now she was here she wasn't so sure. The house looked completely different from the one in the brochure, but she wasn't about to let that ruin her holiday.

The door slammed shut behind her, making her jump, there seemed to be something wrong, maybe it was the flickering light which cast an eerie shadow on the cobwebs, or the fact she felt there was someone or something else present.

She heard a *tap, tap, tap.* Was it the tap dripping? Was it a branch against the window? Or was it blood, dripping from the ceiling? She went to investigate.

The first room she entered was the living room. The stench of mould and damp was so overpowering she could taste it. She advanced to the window, weaving through the cobwebs. The smell was so strong here, she had to cover her nose. She peered out of the window expecting to see a tree against it, but nothing is ever that simple. Instead she saw a silhouette of a man. There was a flash of lightning, just long enough for Lisa to catch the man's features. He was pale, like he'd never seen the sun and his eyes were his most striking feature. They were darker and bigger than your average person's and it seemed unreal.

Lisa was never to be seen again.

Sophie White (14)
Queens College

SAS Operation Goldstud

He turned the corner, his eyes trying to peer through the darkness. He switched on his torch, lifted his rifle and walked into the gloom. Yesterday this building had been a simple bank, but a bank with a secret. A secret so terrible it could completely shatter all politics, peace agreements, weapons trade, everything. This was the 'philosophers legacy' on the outside a simple disk, but the data it held could completely cripple the UK.

Normally the bank was well guarded and populated, but then the government had been sent a message from a man calling himself simply Mr X saying that they had the bank and hostages wanting a reasonable sum for their release. Then he said the only thing possible, 'We will release the legacy to all the world.'

Naturally this worried the government so the Prime Minister had given the word to the military and they sent in the SAS. This is where he came in. He was nervous naturally, but that didn't stop him, he was trained for this. Then he heard it; a shot and he fell to the floor. His squad moved past him unaware of his death. They'd find out but not yet, they had a mission to do and casualties were second to the mission.

Joshua Render (15)
The Arts Educational School

Visions

'I'm having a party. Wanna come?' asked Helen.

'Yeah, OK, I'll be there by 10 because … ' I had a vision. It was the woman behind the counter.

'What is it Kathy?' I saw some oil, burning hot.

'Kathy!' she shook me.

I snapped out of the scary vision. 'What?' I said still thinking about the vision. Then, asking myself I said, 'What would happen if I wasn't snapped out of this scary vision?' I then saw the same woman in my vision. I saw the burning hot oil. I saw the cold water. I realised what was going to happen. She was going to burn herself. I ran as fast as my little legs could take me. '*Stop,*' I said to the woman who was going to be scarred for life. 'You're gonna hurt yourself.'

Confused she looked at me.

'Look, if you don't listen to me you're gonna be scarred for life.'

'Look, I don't know what you're talking about … you're crazy. Just leave me to do my job.'

'But … '

She spilt the cold water. The woman slipped, she tried to recover by getting a grip of the handle of the hot oil. The hot oil spilled on her, she got scarred for life.

After leaving the restaurant, walking down the alley I had another vision.

'Are you OK,' asked Helen.

'I had a vision.'

'What happened?'

'You … were killing … someone.'

'Who? Me? How dare you accuse me of killing someone!'

The person she was killing was me.

Kiera Rhomes (12)
The Arts Educational School

Gunpoint 13

'Happy birthday Leila!' Mum, Dad and Jerry yelled. I grinned and blew out the half melting candles.

'I can't believe that I'm finally ten years old! Not nine, ten!' I laughed and picked up the empty cake box. 'I'll put this in the outdoor bin' I said and bent down to the level of the bin. I dropped the cake box in and stood up. I could feel something hard and circular being rammed painfully into my head. I opened my mouth to scream, but a cold hand covered my mouth. I could only see one thing, a gun! All I saw after that was the word *JAD* painted in white on the gun. *Click, bang, drop,* the world went black.

I woke up what seemed like twenty minutes later. But I wasn't at home. Hospital … how did I get there so quickly? Mum was sobbing on a nurse's shoulder. 'You've been in a coma,' the nurse said, 'for a long time … ' her voice faded into nothing.

'How long has it been?' I asked. 'An hour? A day? A week?'

Mum wailed and suddenly clung to my shoulder. She sniffled and handed me a card. Get well, I expected, but not this time. I couldn't believe it … the card said 'Happy thirteenth birthday'.

Zahra Wynne (11)
The Arts Educational School

Death Seeps Out Of Shadows

Death crept up behind him as he slumbered in the soft cushioned chair. Smoke seeped from Death's cracked, dry lips. Slowly drawing a long, rattling breath cold enough to freeze the soul. A foul-smelling aroma emerged from beneath its worn black hood with an almost deadly, death-defying aura. Placing the still smoking cigarette in his hand. The depth of the omen's heart was cold with mortal loathing, poisoning the soul.

Death struck the match and dropped in onto the arm of the moth-eaten chair, on which the man was sitting. A ring of carmine flames arose, stretching to the now scorched ceiling. Entwining beautiful but deadly saffron and amber outstretched fingers, enclosed around the man as if taking him into a new deadly satanic world, where the dying embers of these flames would never be witnessed. On this occasion, death showed no mercy.

Miss Star-Nox Haydar (13)
The Arts Educational School

The Trench

Saturday 19th May 1915

Today was not the best day ever. It was raining, the mud was up to my knees and half the trench had fallen in. We were sitting ducks from the enemy lines.

Bang! Bang! Bang! They had spotted us. Three bullets whistled above our heads. Me, William, George and Harry dived for cover. There was a cry, someone was hit. It was William, he was hit, dead. It could have been any of us but, no, Death took him.

Wednesday 23rd May

It's a bit lonely without William but I am trying to get it out of my mind. Today we got some terrible news. We found that the trench was never rebuilt and we have to go back to where William died and station our platoon there. All we have is a broken trench for safety.

Saturday 26th May

It has been pouring with rain all day. The mud is like melted chocolate apart from it is cold and watery. The wind is howling and screaming. It is hard to find shelter.

This morning I found a big bite in my diary. Rats. We have seen things in the corners of our eyes. Black things, darting around like black ballerinas. Today our fear came true. Three men fell ill. A plague has come.

Thursday 31st May

Hello, my name is Harry, I was Fred's friend. Before the war we had a party and Fred said if anything happens, you finish my diary. Fred's platoon was the first to go over the top. Fred never came back.

Adam Hagerty (12)
The Arts Educational School

Suicidal

'Hello, how are you? You look pretty today.' 1, 2, 3, 4 …

The flowers on my wall don't talk to me anymore. I knew this would happen sooner or later. No one talks to me anymore, apart from shouting at me, how useless I am. My head, my head, insanity like a fire in my head, burning and boiling *dead, dead, dead!* That's what I want to be. Dead. No more pain, no more talking, no more sadness.

Gasp, what's that noise? The front door, they're home. Should I hide? No, they will find me and then I'd really pay for hiding - my door is flung open.

'Hello …' but just a cold look is my reply. *Bang!* The door closes. I know what's coming next. I can't take another beating. I hear my name mentioned in the distance, drawers opening and closing. I forgot to take the rubbish out. Please God, take me home, back home to my grandmother who loved me, wanted me, cared for me and needed me. I *was* needed, but now I am here with these people who I have to call 'Mummy' and 'Daddy'. I don't even know them, I don't love them and I don't like them.

This must end … the trains; yes that's it.

'Dear Mummy and Daddy, goodbye. I have gone home'.

The walk was foggy and cold. I could hear the trains coming but I couldn't see it. 1, 2, 3, 4 … what if I don't die, they'll kill me. The note!

Renée Ocran (12)
The Arts Educational School

How About A New Beginning?

He did it again, but this time it was on my face, last time it was on my back.

It all started when I was little, just a small smack on the arm when I was being rude, but I'm fourteen now and he's still doing it, but worse.

The bruise on my face covered half my lip and my eye. All of this, just for being me. I wish, I just wish my mum was here, but he hit her too - that's why she left.

'You got any homework?' Dad said in a harsh voice.

'Yes, I can do my maths, but I need help with English.'

'Well get on and do it, you little brat.'

The look on his face will give me nightmares for a long time. I could sense he was going to hit me. It was the look saying, 'what did you just say you naughty girl'. But just then he smiled. A flood of relief ran through me. Then it happened. *Punch! Slap!* Stinging pain.

I ran upstairs crying so hard I felt sick.

'You stupid, stupid girl!' Dad screamed, throwing a plate on the ground. I had had enough. I ran out of the front door, I could still hear him from way down the street.

'I can't do this anymore,' I said to myself. I ran to the park and slumped onto the bench. But a large dark figure caught the corner of my eye. It was a massive oak tree. All I needed was some rope.

'How about a new beginning?'

Isabel McClelland (12)
The Arts Educational School

Looking For Daddy

Sick dripped from my lips as I struggled for breath in the cubical. My teeth felt like acid and my throat was ragged, sore and dry. I banged my head against the back of the cubical door, tears falling from my eyes like raindrops on a winter's day. I flushed the toilet and went to wash my mouth out.

'Lils, you there?' It was my friend Sally. I hadn't told her yet about my bulimia but I had a strong feeling that she had been suspecting something.

'Lils, what are you doing in there? You missed all … ' she saw me crying into my lap in the corner of the rotting bathroom. 'Oh my God, look at you,' she cried holding my small bony arm.

I wiped my face and snuffled, 'I … I … I can't help it,' I said, bursting into tears. 'Dad's death has driven Mum …' I struggled for words, 'mad. And Mandy, she's only five, she wants Dad back, so do I.'

Sally led me to the sink and told me to wash out my mouth and eyes. Then she gave me some mints and put her arm around me like I was her baby. I wish I was.

That very night I was on a bridge overhanging the deep murky river. Mum didn't need me anymore, nobody did. And the only person who ever appreciated me for who I really was had been Dad. So I decided to join him, my daddy.

Imogen Waterhouse (11)
The Arts Educational School

Who, Who Wasn't There?

'Mama,' I called, 'why is she screaming?'

I know why. Mama is trying to put Isi in a corset … again. I shouldn't refer to her as Isi, Your Highness would be better.

'Robin, is she ready?'

Who is that?

'No,' I called back. It must be her fiancé but how does he know my name? How does he know I exist? It said, 'Isi is much too fair for her fiancé'. I couldn't stop myself from crying. 'But she is marrying him today. The king is forcing her. Now tell me who you are?'

There was no reply. I kept asking but all I can hear are my silent tears, my silent cries. I will call him Who, who wasn't there.

Here she is. Dressed in white, Crying. Each teardrop sparkling in the moonlight once, before falling on the grass. Just like me. Except I walked on waves; like a ghost at midnight. To die. To escape from him. Now I watch my little sister doing the same as me. This time with a corset to suffocate her. She has drawn her last breath. I would stop her but Who, Who was not there. And I am Who and Robin.

Two minds, now three. My sister and me. And Who; my courage who wasn't there.

Alice White (12)
The Arts Educational School

Darkness

The stone floor was cold and ancient, it reminded me of Granny, because of its colour, a pottery-rich red she said I was very lucky. However something was telling me that right now I was the furthest thing away from lucky; being trapped in this dungeon, with skulls and spiders waiting to scare you everywhere you turn and shadows filling in all the corners, this could easily be described as my worst nightmare!

Slowly and carefully I edged my way to my feet, making sure I didn't even make the sound of a pin dropping to the floor. I grabbed one of the torches that lit the halls (which was scary, because they looked as if they were waiting to fall down and squash me).

I decided to go down a dark cave, hoping I could escape, but my ruffled brown hair collected many surprises such as cobwebs, moss, rotten water, but phew did it stink!

The sole of my shoe padded on every step I now took onto the thick cobbled sand. I looked up to notice the light had now vanished and a thick jet-black cloud had covered me, now the only thing that kept me going in the right direction, was this slowly burning out candle.

All of a sudden my bones turned to ice, a long icy wind, shivered down my spine.

… Out of nowhere, a paw the size of me lay in front of me, as shadows and blood scarred the terrifying scales!

Daisy Hampton (12)
The Arts Educational School

To The Past

I was walking to school, it was a regular day. But today wasn't a normal day. Today I found a fifty pound note. It wasn't a typical fifty pound note with Queen Elizabeth II on it, it was King Henry VIII as King in 1509. 1509 was the year Henry was given the throne and became king.

When I finished school and went home I just watched this fifty pound note. I was lying on my bed and my eyes began to get heavier and heavier and before I knew it, I was asleep. When I woke up I was in a king-sized bed and someone called out the words, 'Anne, my love, are you awake?'

I shot up and got out of bed and said, 'Oh yes my darling.'

My ladies-in-waiting washed me, dressed me and did my hair. Henry and I went to a parliament meeting. When we got back home to Hampton Court Palace Henry spoke to me in the waiting chamber and said that I had been cheating on him. Henry sentenced me to death.

Two days after we spoke, I was due to die. I was scared and it was a cold day. My ladies-in-waiting put on an extra layer over my clothes. I walked up the guillotine and saw another fifty pound note with Queen Elizabeth II on it. I picked it up and I was in my bedroom.

Kym Alexander (13)
The Arts Educational School

Him

I still don't know why he did it. It is unexplainable. My sister died last week, and in our house too. I know who killed her. I just can't get round to turning him in. I see him every day. I used to be quite close to him but I don't feel that way anymore. He had always been so trustworthy, till now …

What will happen if I tell the police? Will he know it was me? Will he threaten me … or worse?

I saw him this morning. Looking innocent.

He looked innocent that day too. Mum was out. Julie and I were on the sofa. He came in. I went out. I came back and she was dead. I panicked, I was startled. I rang Mum. She came back, rang 999. Police everywhere; but only I knew.

I'm scared. I feel sick. I can't hold this secret for much longer. I need someone to talk to. There is a saying 'a problem shared is a problem halved'. I don't have anyone to share mine with though. My best friend was my sister and now she is gone.

The police had to question us all of course. 'Routine enquiries' they call it.

I am going to tell them soon. I don't know when, but soon. I think he will go to jail and he will always hate me. Scary thing is, maybe my mum will too.

I will always need two parents, but now I can only ever have one.

Billie Hylton (12)
The Royal School Hampstead

Death Is Just The Beginning

Creak went the cellar door then laughter from a woman. Woken by the noise Clair walked slowly down the stairs. The lady's voice was familiar, but not from the family. The cellar door was open. The laughter began and then a loud scream scared Clair. A shiver went up her spine. Whispers began saying, 'Clair'. Then a photo on the wall fell to the ground. The photo showed Clair and her family. A hammer fell on top of the photo then the hammer returned to its place. Out of Clair in the photo blood came out. She went closer to see, then blood squirted out, she slipped and cried, screamed. She covered her face with her hands, the blood disappeared. The lights turned off. Clair stood up, she looked up and saw the moon. Suddenly a strong force pushed her to a grave.

It read: *Monalisa Secarto, Beloved sister and daughter 1985-2002.*

That's my baby-sitter I thought she went back to Brazil, thought Clair. Then a scream at the same time Clair was pushed to another grave.

It read: *Clair Carlson, No one ?-2006.*

Clair's mouth dropped. Suddenly a hand grabbed Clair under the earth. Clair's parents and sister stood there watching her curled on the floor screaming and crying at the sight. She clutched the hammer tightly, if anyone touched her Clair would hit them with the weapon. Then quickly Clair opened her eyes. They had turned red. Blood. With the weapon she beat her family to their death.

Anxhela Koci (12)
The Royal School, Hampstead